CORPUS CHRISTI, TEXAS

†

CRUZ DEL CASTILLO

This edition first published in paperback by
Michael Terence Publishing in 2023
www.mtp.agency

Copyright © 2023 Cruz Del Castillo

Cruz Del Castillo has asserted the right to be identified as
the author of this work in accordance with the
Copyright, Designs and Patents Act 1988

ISBN 9781800946118

Cover photography
Sophie Klampferer

Cover design
Dasha Davidyuk

Michael Terence
Publishing

To my Texan cousin, Cecilia.
My best friend and soul mate for life.
This is for us and the battles we have both endured.

Contents

FOREWORD

Fever Dream
by Iñaki Aguilar Lomelí

If you can't kill them in person, kill them with a piece of paper and a fountain pen

I had a dream last night where I had coffee with my past English literature tutor. We were sitting in the middle of the Bluebird Cafe at a lopsided wooden table. The place was empty, left forsaken and abandoned like the lilac-patterned cashmere sweater vest my grandfather left on the back of his drawer when he mercilessly died out of breath. The space was excruciatingly sombre and grey, like the dried-out flower bouquet my theatre director once gave me after I performed my hare-brained and unreformed cabaret. Pitch-black, no light, darkness and shadows engulfed every pickle and corner of this uninhibited space. Despite the woollen blindfold the environment had placed around my eyes with such rigidity, and tightness that I could almost feel the throbbing sensation of blood pumping from my heart travelling all the way to the veins of my brain in the back of my head, I was still surprisingly able to see and smell everything with such specific detail and comprehension. I carefully observed how the chilly brisk gust of wind coming from the opened door of the interior made the cobwebs in the corners of the place gingerly sway. I was scarcely frightened by those meagre strong-boned arachnids and tarantulas trying to seduce me, as they slowly danced and frolicked through their hand-crafted weaves with their hairy, scraggy pedipalps. The putridly brutish dust and growling grime collected between the stilted floorboards annoyingly blocked my dainty nostrils, making me unable to breathe as glutinous mucus accumulated down my throat and swelled the alveoli of my lungs.

The incarnation and aphrodisiac embodiment of Professor John Keating sat right in front of me. His lips were tied with some tight black thread interweaved through the margins of his muzzle. And his eyes were as shut and closed as the wooden and bloodless heart of that lanky French ginger-bearded straight man from Marseille, who kissed me on the dance floor that one occasional night out in Dalston and made me cry in the cubicles

3

of those dirty bathrooms all night long. My English teacher, who had Robin Williams' visage printed on his face, in this vicious and constructed reality, looked as scared as the heterosexual twat I met at my high school library, who secretly took me to the third floor's disabled toilets, and kissed and fucked me uncontrollably with his feisty hands covering the screams that came out of my mouth. I found myself lost and deserted in the ghost town of my own unconsciousness. A fever dream I wished to carefully decrypt, and meticulously debunk, like trying to untangle my apple-wired earphones after they had been crumpled up in a ball all the way at the end of my trousers' pocket for more than a year. Nevertheless, I was still unable to comprehend or gauge why the train of my thoughts kept drifting and going off their own rails. On the flip side of the coin, the old and kindred spirit whose words were wise, sat static and still on his chair, unable to move a finger or shake an arm, like the last vegetable left on the grocery patch; or like the retired bones and muscles of my uncle, when he savagely flew out of the front seat of his car into the highway in that one painful and excruciating accident. The man that once used to lecture me and all of my other two-faced disciples had suddenly lost the power to speak or teach about the pain of falling in love. All of those John Keats odes and poems I used to bathe over had turned me into the double-edged sword, hopeless romantic he wanted all of us to become.

The moles on his veiny, bony hands spoke to me through their own intricate, convoluted constellations. He was being held hostage against his will, the same way my feelings for men were imprisoned and tortured in a heteronormative, patriarchal dungeon until the age of eighteen. I still remember that moment when he consoled me under the fluorescent lights of cold glacial school corridors. The point in time where I stormed out of the classroom crying because someone had created a rumour that I ruined my ex-best friend's life. Like 'Telephone' or 'Chinese whispers', all of these hypocritical voices had invented that I reported her to the police, and wanted to take her to court for trespassing my *own* house when she was trying to seek vengeance that one Saturday morning. He said, "The bravest thing you can ever do in life is to leave the person you feared losing the most behind." So, I let go of the rope that kept straining the palm of my hands and said goodbye to the sour friendship that used to corrode and oxidise my ginger golden bones into moss-grown bronze.

The heat that throbbed inside of my head started to increase and intensify the visions and apparitions as they became louder and more bombastically prominent. I no longer found myself in the deteriorated and decayed Bluebird Cafe with my English teacher and his ill-hearted liver. But in a room full of broken mirrors with someone's shadow I recognised gleaming upon me. I could smell that musty breath, and its eminent notes of rotten tobacco and marinated burnt-up coffee. It was him. The man who vulgarly touched my body illegally back in the autumn of twenty-seventeen. The man who had once promised to erase the depression and anxiety from my system. The man who asked me to take my trousers off and show him my erections. The man who masked his physical and sexual abuse as some sort of 'Taoist' practice. The man who forced me to lay on that sofa butt naked. The man who used to check the door lock more than three times to avoid anyone witnessing how he brutishly breathed on me. The man who took my purity and innocence away. The man I have always had the desire to kill with my own, bare, gritty hands. The man who deserved to be emasculated for his crimes. The man who deserved to be hanged. The man who deserved to be castrated. The man who turned me into a Misandrist Beau. The *man* who deserved to be wiped out of the existence of this planet.

I had never thought of killing anyone before, but the rage and anger took out the primitive beast inside of me, as if it were trying to reclaim its own dreary childhood back. You can do anything you want in lucid dreaming without facing any type of consequences, or at least that is what my psychology teacher said in that class we had about sociopaths and serial killers. But why would anyone want to incarcerate me for seeking justice and murdering my own abuser? So, I did what I had been waiting to do my entire life since he last touched me: to kill him.

Like a beautiful, mystical pagan ritual, all of those beautifully broken mirrors witnessed his demise and watched how I tried to regain my despondent, molested teenagehood back. I grabbed him tightly by the neck and spat on his face. He was trying to fight back, like a Doberman dog. His wrinkly, prune-like face was going scarlet red. He tried to gasp for air, like a gazelle in the African Savanna, trying to reach the surface of the water but getting brutishly drowned and mangled by a crocodile. As grit and courage peaked my bloodstream, I quickly grabbed a shard from the floor and punctured his malevolent eyeballs as his sullen and bitter blood splattered on my chest. I was slaying the dragon, beheading it, saving the town of my own being. After a few moments, I stood up, tasted my victory, and observed how his corpse vulgarly drooled his gutter into its own smutty blood pool.

The mirrors were clapping, audible cheers, I got a standing ovation from the audience who watched the scene; an apocalyptical and primitive Aztec human sacrifice. They were all smiling with tears streaming down their faces, and couldn't stop applauding with their exasperated sore hands. Like a Metropolitan Hero without a flying cape, I had saved everyone and myself from his unwashed and filthy crimes. His shadow was finally unable to walk behind mine, and his smell at long last had stopped permeating the pores of my epidermis. I stoically ordered Jesus to send him to the gates of hell and begged the Devil to pull the limbs and extremities of his body with tight ropes in order to tear his perverted bones apart. Something magical happens when you stop giving a fuck, so I grabbed the keys of his crimson cherry-red Maserati and brutally crashed it in the church he used to go to every Sunday with his family. I no longer was the victim of these male half-breeds and their fucking stupid games; I was the vengeful vigilante saviour castrating men at midnight who kept touching their partners non-consensually and fucked their misters and mistresses in the backseat of their wife's car.

Nonetheless, irrational fears still consumed and plagued my

mind. I was too afraid of living my life as his victim, frightened by the idea that I wouldn't be able to stop writing about him. I was extremely terrified by the thought of his ghostly hands beneath my bed pulling me down to the ground when I sleepwalked in the middle of the night. I was petrified to see his reflection in my tarnished mirror whenever I would want to look at my bare naked body. I was scared to hear his name in public and get aroused by it. I was flustered to accept the fact that he put his finger up my own arse. But as my therapist always used to say, "Your biggest fears will always chase you down even if you try to get rid of them." I pondered on those words, contemplating their meaning, and how they applied to my life. I killed him in an attempt to dispose of his criminal presence from my past, but like stabbing a ghost, a knife can only puncture through thin air. Be that as it may, in the real world, outside of our bizarre and outlandish fantasies, acceptance and inaction will always be the harsh and penetrating truth in one's life. You *must* learn to let go of the people who wanted to see you die. I now rinse my skin with chamomile foam in the bath every night, trying to remind myself that *my body* no longer belongs to him.

My broken soul and brain kept asking me questions my fever dream was unable to answer. My motionless body lay asleep on the mattress and bed sheets I once lovingly wetted with my sweat and semen. The bed where the man I thought I'd marry one day had drilled me from the back with the romance of his callous and throbbing phallus, right before the Friday he fucked this ugly wench in the Salsa Campeche Club in central, when I was in the crowded bathroom throwing all my juices up. Like the shape and composition of that night's vomit, my thoughts kept splattering and splashing into the windshield of my existence and made my sleeping corpse severely twitch and tremble.

I now choose my men like I choose my foods on the aisles of organic grocery stores. I like expensive shit with pure and clean ingredients. However, the intoxicating and radioactive-looking Flaming Hot Cheetos are hard to resist and make my mouth water the same way the manlike vulture in my phone makes my

7

spinal cords tingle and sends my heart into a frozen-like beat when he sends me a picture of his protruding naked bulge with no grudge through his pathetic fake Instagram account. I like to drink the fervent pineapple juice their hairy chests sweat and excrete when their bodies are all over me, whilst they clutch my hands tightly behind my head, like a steam room whispering in my ears. I no longer like to play the submissive and weak. I make them cry their own exuberance through their eyes and make them work as hard as they can. I am the regal and majestic marble sculpture, and they are the overworked sculptors. I like to go to bed knowing that I am their most extravagant highly priced possession when they grip my body tight, and puncture my clavicle with their prickly, sharp chin, and hug their chest closely against my underweight back at midnight. But he had the curse of the wolf, when the clock struck twelve.

I found myself sitting on that bench in the park in Mexico again. Back on April 30th, 2020 amid the pandemic when every little soul and creature was ruthlessly dying. I could still recall the stench of that dreadful cold, and how both of our heads were soaked, and our clothes drenched and revoked. The memory of how your sexy, muscular ogre-like hands stroked the cheeks of my face made me sharply scratch the side of my legs. I used to send you pictures for you to view of how I made my thighs leak and bleed to the thought of you. The way you looked at me with your devil-like gaze and made me yearn for all of your scorching dog days was truly improper and unfair. Darkness gleamed upon us. But we were both masochists who loved to burn our skins with lustful fire. All I knew is that I wanted you, someone to forget to. All you wanted was to play, but honey, this wasn't a game. Your intricacy and perplexity, you had this all schemed and measured. I could see the venom leaking from your lips, and how I craved it so badly that I licked it off your cheeks. Was this love? Or just lust? Was I desperate? Or just utterly broken? I was so ready to feast like a broken-hearted beast just so I could forget about the ungodly and profane affair I had with that German priest.

The number on the scale kept invading all of my lullaby-stricken dreams. I hate to think that there are still people in my life that still believe that my struggles with food and my body are just for glittery shows. Someone called me dramatic the other day and said I didn't look that sick and skinny, others told me to stop posting my running kilometres on my stories, and some others got upset when I dumped my chicken Caesar salad down the drain and documented it on my Instagram's close friends. But I still cry when I see my stomach lumps fold one on top of the other, and I still hyperventilate when I am no longer able to see my ribs when I breathe deeply in front of the mirror. I could see myself juggling clubs in a trapeze in the middle of a rodeo with clown paint all over my face, smiling my way through all that pain, almost as if this recovery journey was being taken as a farce and a ruthless joke. If only I could tell every single one of them how scary it was for me to see how I went from seventy-five to fifty-six kilograms in a few weeks, back when I used to weigh myself in front of the mirror and would secretly log my weight on the notes app of my phone every morning. I wish I could scream at their big-nosed faces and explain how I had to keep my head down whilst walking through the corridors of my mendacious hypocritical university. The chilling and daunting feeling that used to completely consume and wrench the insides of my body. I can still anxiously recall that moment when one of my teachers saw me at the university's forum after the Christmas break and the way his jaw dropped all the way down to the floor. I became this unfathomable phantom out of thin air. He struggled to talk or open his mouth. *"What happened to you?"* he mumbled. *"Your face looks so different,"* he muttered. *"You've lost so much weight,"* he muffled. *"You've lost like two stones,"* he stammered. *"How did you do that?"* he inquired. *"What type of diet are you on?"* he strikingly interrogated. Luckily enough, I didn't have to say anything in order for him to shut his *fucking* mouth up. I killed him with one look and uncomfortably walked away.

"BOOM!" Just like that. My brain had savagely exploded. The timer of the rent-free grenade that lived inside my skull had finally gone off. My newly decorated room with Native

American-made bohemian carpets, well-watered plants, Lana del Rey posters, and dainty fairy lights that shape-shifted my space into a magical firefly land, had turned into a dismantled and obliterated no man's land. Debris and broken cement pieces took down all of the prints and pictures on my walls and demolished the frame with the photograph of my beautiful youthful mother holding me as a new-born baby. The smell of smoke had eradicated my trademarked scent of lavender incense. White swan feathers slowly swayed and danced through the air as broken glass from the shattered windows deflated my drowsy swan-feathered white linen duvet. My room's unrelenting roof and ceiling were no longer existent. My frail and naked body lay on the wooden tiles of my cold-blooded floor, like the dead fox I saw on the pavement whilst running in Finchley Road last Thursday. All of the memories I had once cherished metamorphosed into the cremated ashes of the people I used to love. Hollow-headed, my pulsating broken-down brain lay beside my throbbing head, diced into pieces, beating on its own. All of a sudden, out of nowhere, my body started levitating into thin air, a string pulling me up from the centre of my stomach. I was a beheaded marionette. Jesus grabbed and huddled my weak and frail corpse from the floor of my room to the Elysian Fields up above the sky with his colossal, and gargantuan hands. Like a UFO abducting one of those corpulent cows in the middle of the night from their farms in those eighties sci-fi films my father used to let me watch with him in the middle of the night, in that Orlando motel, two highways away from Disney World.

An oleaginous, nipple-less, naked woman happily received me on the golden gates of heaven as she tightly pressed her corrugated breast against my bony chest. *'I shouldn't have indulged in those mind-bending and psychotropic brownies with Skylar before bed, last night.'* I thought to myself. Trying to remind my brain that this is only a dream. These barbaric and ruthless psychedelics had consequently and majestically rearranged the organs inside of my body and had shrewdly recalibrated the neurones of my anxious nervous system. But I guess that was *exactly* what I needed. As I floated in the cotton-candied clouds, I started to fervently touch the thing between my legs and rained all over the cities that had physically destroyed me in the past. Baptising their outlawed nefarious citizens with the smell and taste of my pain and hurt. Unrepentant, I relentlessly drowned all the inhabitants of these cities with a ruthless and merciless tsunami as I pleasured myself to the thought of Matt (a theatre director that had secretly fucked me in his canal boat home in the river near Paddington Railway Station in the winter of the second COVID-19 lockdown). I visualised him opening my back and cutting the ribs of my spine, like the pagan rituals the Vikings used to perform on their most hated enemies in pre-medieval Scandinavia.

If I fuck the men I love, and the men I love fuck *me*, then why is my life full of unrequited love stories? I can still hear the croaky whispers in the corridors of my house of that Italian young man from southern Italy I kissed at the age of seventeen when I walk bare naked from my bedroom to the bathroom in the middle of the night. I still haven't been able to wash my hair or brush my teeth since he last imprinted his alcoholic, and cannabis-filled breath on my lips on that birthday bash I turned eighteen. I thought he was mine, but I was *never* his. Although embarrassingly sentimental and melodramatic, I still cry to this very day every time I watch Titanic. Especially the scene where Rose Dewitt Bukater lets go of Jack Dawson after he freezes to death in the glacial, heartless Atlantic Ocean. It selfishly brings me back to that moment: the twenty-fifth of March when I saw him going through those airport security gates in Heathrow Terminal Five. The moment when I knew I would never, *ever,* see him again. I left the city in which we were first conceived right after. I left the room with the sheets, the bed where he first devoured me. I carried the burden, on my back, until the end of time, and said goodbye to Room Number Sixteen in the student accommodation I used to live in Princes Square. I left the walls of that room tainted, and unwashed, with all of those hurtful intimate experiences and hot-blooded anecdotes we had both shared. Presently, even though the planet has fully rotated around the sun more than four times since I last saw him, I still have his socks and underwear he once gave me before he left, sealed in a plastic bag with his smell, kept in the back of my drawer.

I miss the fragility I once used to possess when I was sixteen. I miss 'Samuel'. The twenty-two-year-old Australian blue-eyed hunk whom I lost my virginity to in the summer of 2019 in Madrid, back when I was reckless and I lied to him about my age and told him I was eighteen, when really, I was *sixteen*. Unlike many of my other friends' 'first-time' stories, my 'first', 'true', 'the one I called my first time even though it wasn't (because my therapist couldn't keep his hands to himself a few years before)' first time, *was the best sex I have ever had in my life*. Samuel held my thighs and arms like a prized possession. Samuel rubbed his wet lips through my skin like he truly loved me. Even though he was older, and the age gap between us was scary and disturbing, and I had conned him about my age, Samuel had been the only man in my life at that point that had treated me like the royal blue prince I *truly* was. Samuel respected and admired my body like a foreign tourist eulogizing Michelangelo's David in the 'Accademia Gallery' in Florence. Samuel kissed me with such fragility and passion. I still remember opening my eyes and catching a glimpse of his face and thinking, *'I never want this moment to end.'* Samuel walked me to the Atocha Train Station near the Reina Sofia Museum in the middle of the night after we had spent the whole afternoon in his bedroom. Samuel kissed my lips goodbye. Samuel released my hands as I passed through the barriers to go catch my train. Samuel left. I never saw or heard from him ever again.

I hardly cry now. I don't laugh that much either. Although Fluoxetine altered the chemical imbalance within my brain to make me want to live, it has also drained my sensitivity and emotions from the entirety of my veins. I *thankfully*, no longer pace Waverley Grove at midnight in my black baggy Fruit of the Loom zip up hoodie, and a pair of caramel-scuffed Birkenstock clogs with the phone in my hand shaking; thinking of what could be the least painful way to kill myself. I *now* lie in bed at 2AM, under the dreamy fairy lights I hung between my paper-white walls, listening to Lana del Rey in slowed and reverb with my

Koss Porta Pro Beige headphones. I eat the juicy, succulent, cotton candy grapes I *proudly* stole from M&S and stare at the ceiling. I masturbate to the thought of finally being able to be happy. I no longer want to be the one who stands out from the crowd, the person that used to wear lavishly-woven fur coats. Or the wannabe indie boy who used to dress in vintage baker boy hats and Harris Tweed jackets. Or the foolish Harry Styles impersonator that would walk into the classroom with a Vegas-like, neon-coloured feathered boa around his neck, and long white silk gloves on his arms. I *now* just want to breathe. I just want to exist. I *simply* just want to live.

It is time to reclaim my power and strength and quit victimising my own pain. I have a passion for romanticising my suffering, my sadness, my heartache, my grief, my wretchedness, my hardship, the list goes on. Having said that, I think this is the only way I have learnt to cope with these traumas. I sugar-coat these uncomfortable, adverse feelings and experiences into something that exists beyond the boundaries of my own broken heart. I like to imagine I am some sort of misunderstood or betrayed protagonist in a piece of literature or film, and everybody is voyeuristically watching my own pain and sorrow unfold right in front of them. Maybe this could be a sign of something bigger, of something more complex. Maybe I am just asking for mercy or sympathy. Maybe my lungs and throat are already tired of screaming. Maybe this romanticised emotional hurt and anguish are fabricated by my own superior self; constructed by the mastermind of a nineteenth-century romantic author. As the Croatian guy I used to casually hook up with in quarantine once told me, "Your pain feels measured, controlled and displayed to the public like the penis of Michelangelo's David." And maybe he *is* right. Maybe I have forced myself to write hurtful and vulnerable passages like these because I idealise and glamourise the way John Keats and Virginia Woolf used to write about the monsters that used to live rent-free inside their heads. Or maybe I also aspire to be a cultural figure like Jack Kerouac and be a part of something bigger, like the way the Beat Generation would advocate for personal release, purification, and illumination, against the backdrop of New York City's Greenwich Village in the nineteen-fifties.

I haven't been socially meandering lately. I am no longer petrified to miss out on any party or social gathering. I pleasantly suffer from a new phenomenon called 'ROMO', which stands for: 'Relief of Missing Out', the binary opposition to 'FOMO', which stands for: 'Fear of Missing Out.' I keep cancelling all of my plans. I cancel them at the last minute and give no explanations. I am learning to say 'no', and I am succeeding. My twenty-first birthday is coming up soon on the first of March and I solely want to spend it alone with my pen and paper and the beautiful sound of my Taylor Swift and Lana del Rey vinyl records. I have learnt to stop expecting things from people. I have accepted that the men I used to love that broke my heart didn't owe me anything, and that they still don't. I realised that all of my heartbreaks have been my own fault and my own doing. I recognised that I was the one to blame for my own pain. I let these men walk right over me with their rugged muddy tractors because I felt worthless and inferior, and I thought that was what I truly deserved. I stopped lending my whole life to meaningless men who made me feel special one night and then would cruelly dispose of me into the junkyard of the anal-fissured twinks the morning after. I finally acknowledged my own worth. I deleted all those idiotic and foolish dating apps where one has to sell their own carcass and body as a product. I stopped marketing my physique like the Dyson vacuum advertisement that used to vulgarly interrupt my SpongeBob SquarePants show I used to watch every night after school when I was five in my fluffy dinosaur onesie, whilst I gingerly ate my sugar-topped, cream cheese toast. I no longer let small talks with random guys from the internet drift into a dreary and emotionless make-out session in their ugly sublet apartments, which clearly lacked 'real love' or substance. The thought of being and *staying* alone, surprisingly enough, arouses me.

Although the Tennessee Williams inside of me wouldn't like to end this on a cheerful and happy note, a fever dream has to conclude with a '*and he lived happily ever after*', the same way the sun will always shine after a hefty storm. Having said that, I am delighted to tell you that this delirious and frenzied dream ends on a warm-hearted summer night in mid-July in the middle of a high-grassed wheat field, in the spheres of freedom where I can take all my clothes off and artfully undress. The sun starts to set. Sensually touching its own horizon. The skies turn from a blue to a dark orange-pink hue. I hysterically scream and aggressively howl at the wind. I start dancing, jumping in circles, allowing my genitals to swing back and forth. I let myself go crazy. I accept that I am deranged. I laugh. I cry. I cackle. I moan. I am reeling from my open wounded heart. I am healing. Like Dionysus, the God of wine and pleasure, I party with myself and Mother Nature until the dawn of time. I am finally free. And I have finally woken up, from this wild, feral, untamed, chaotic, primitive, tempestuous, *fever dream.*

Iñaki Aguilar Lomelí
February 21st, 2023

PART ONE

1 Peter 5:8

*"Be alert and of sober mind.
Your enemy the devil prowls around
like a roaring lion looking for someone to devour."*

Prologue

Isaiah 53:7

"He was oppressed and afflicted,
yet he did not open his mouth;
he was led like a lamb to the slaughter,
and as a sheep before its shearers is silent,
so he did not open his mouth."

There is always an aspect of sadness and an unexplained bittersweet melancholia that comes with the beginning of summer. The rays of sunlight that shine through the shutters of my window in the morning mercilessly pierce through my skin and force me to feel somehow cheerful and positive, encouraging me to go outside and seize the day. But in reality, all I want to do is to bury myself under my whitewashed cotton linen covers and reminisce about the time he forcefully pinned my arms behind my head and aggressively thrusted his penis inside of me at 'La Santa Espina' motel.

The beginning of summer means I have to go back to my hometown in Corpus Christi, Texas. To my culture. To my community. To my religion. To my family's tradition. To my parents. And to my upbringing. My deceased grandparents, Rosa and Antonio, immigrated to Texas about fifty-five years ago from Hermosillo, Mexico. Antonio was a pastor, and with his wife, Rosa, they created what is known today as: 'El Cuerpo de Cristo' church. In the 1960s it became the largest Hispanic church run by Mexican immigrants in Corpus Christi. And ever since, it has stayed as the most prolific and renowned Mexican Catholic church in our city. My mother, Juanito, Carlos and Cristobal (her older brothers), and Angela (her younger sister) have all been baptised, have all been given the Sacrament of the Holy Eucharist for the first time, have all been confirmed, and have all

19

been married to their heteronormative partners under the roof of this church. The earliest, most crisp memory I have in 'El Cuerpo de Cristo' is from when I was a baby and Father Francisco accidentally dropped me inside the baptismal font in my baptism. I still remember the high-pitched sound of my whole family's gasp and how it echoed all throughout the interior of the church. My life has been built and destroyed time after time from my childhood to my teenage years within the incarcerating boundaries of this establishment.

The first time I was ever labelled *'a black sheep'* in my life was when I was five years old, and I was forced to go to Sunday school by my mother like all my other younger family members. Every Sunday, children of my same age group from the town would gather in the office complex above the church at 10AM before mass to learn about the Bible, God, and Jesus. I hated Sunday school. I hated how cold the place was. The air conditioner had a musty, mouldy smell that knotted and swelled my throat. The fluorescent lights that hung above the frail wooden desks were stark and uninviting. The children were loud and clingy. They all talked to each other but avoided talking to me. My older cousins used to tell the other kids that I was weird, that I was different, but I didn't even know why. Until one day Mother Carmen took me outside the classroom and told me that my heart was going to rot like a rotten wretched apple if I kept sinning. But I didn't know what my sins were and how she knew of them. A few years later, my mother brutally confessed to me in a merciless heated discussion that she and my father were extremely worried for me because I allegedly used to be very interested in the Devil as a child.

When Mother Carmen told us the story of the Devil in Sunday school for the first time, I felt mesmerised and understood. I liked the character and how it went against everything and everyone, especially God himself. I mischievously started to talk about the Devil with the children in the lunch breaks and fantasised about a life with him. Mother Carmen forbade us to mouth the word *'Devil'*. We were to refer to him as

'El Angel Caído' or *'El D'*. Mother Carmen was strong-willed and stubborn. There were no exceptions. If you were to disobey her, you were to get brutally punished. That is how the church had always worked since they started to burn the witches in the inquisition in the Middle Ages. But I liked mouthing the word *'Diablo'*, especially because of the reaction I would get from the other children. They would get scared and startled and would run straight to Mother Carmen crying. Consequently, I was suspended from Sunday school and never returned. I ridiculed my whole family; people didn't understand how the grandson of the founder of *'El Cuerpo de Cristo'* could be preaching about the Devil in such a fervent and passionate manner. But I was only five and the Bible was just another stupid fairy-tale to me. I liked antagonists. I liked villains. I liked the character that the Devil played in the Bible. So, I became his closeted number one cult follower. I never took the religion that was shoved excruciatingly down my throat since I was yanked out of my mother's vagina seriously. And although my negligent attitude towards their religion had been a huge frustration and let down within my whole immediate family, I was still forced to finish Sunday school on my own and do my First Communion and Confirmation.

The word *'Homosexual'* was equally as frightening and blood-curdling as the word *'Devil'* inside my household, almost as if they were both synonyms. My parents were always afraid I was a homosexual when I was a child because of my effeminate manners and feminine interests, in comparison to my older twin brothers' virile and masculine dividends. However, no one ever confronted me head-on about it. They were too afraid that it could be true, and I was too.

The first time I realised I did in fact like boys was when I was thirteen and I found a magazine of naked women hidden inside the chest of drawers of my brother Mario. The big meaty breasts and vaginas inside the magazine scared me, and somewhat repelled me. Nevertheless, I still wanted to like them and forced myself to feel attracted to them. So, I tried touching myself down there whilst I looked at their bodies, and even though it had been my first time stroking my penis that way, I didn't feel anything down there. I couldn't even get hard. I felt extremely unfulfilled and unsatisfied. But at the same time scared and frightened to accept that I was in fact a homosexual. My parents' worst nightmare.

Jesus Christ was the first man I ever masturbated to. I still have a very vivid memory of that sexual awakening. I remember tearing my trousers off my legs aggressively and getting on my bed on all fours. I closed my eyes and imagined Jesus grabbing my body from behind. With his long hair and scabrous beard tickling me, kissing my neck and sensually tracing the skin of my cheeks with his coarse dry lips. I savagely ripped the picture frame of Jesus that sacredly hung on the wall above my headboard and viciously kissed it. I started hyperventilating and became light-headed. My limbs and extremities rapidly trembled. I took my penis out of my cotton blue striped boxers and nastily caressed it. I stared at Jesus directly into his jade green eyes and tainted his picture with my pure innocent juvenile semen. Jesus was the reason why I had fallen in love with rugged and bearded men, and ever since I tarnished his picture with my yearning lustful bodily fluids, I have been a walking blasphemy. From that moment on, I had been awaiting impatiently for a man with long hair, emerald, green eyes and a scruffy unkempt beard to take my virginity away. But that man never came.

The first time I lost my virginity was when I was fifteen, and it wasn't to Jesus or to the long-haired-green-eyed-bearded man I had made up in my mind. It was to Father Orlando. I have been in denial for far too many years and have tried to erase every happenstance from my mind, whilst not succeeding in any way. No one ever knew that I was a victim of this self-assertive crime, and I will never be able to tell anyone about it either. It was hard to accept that the foulest and ugliest man in the realm of this world was the first man that took my sexuality, freedom and autonomy away from me. Father Orlando's breath smelled worse than a medieval brothel plagued by syphilis and gonorrhoea, or an ancient rotten wet market filled with dead animal corpses.

Father Orlando's face was reminiscent of that of a Gargoyle. His eyes were small but evil. His forehead was bigger than the respect he had for me. His head was hairless, otherworldly, almost alien-like and embarrassingly cone-shaped. His hands were big and ogre-like grotesque. Father Orlando was fat and sluggish, lumps of flesh and corpulence hung and dangled from his waistline to the floor. Father Orlando smelled like raw meat. Father Orlando smelled like the underworld. Father Orlando smelled like the Devil. Father Orlando was the Devil, or at least that is what I used to think. Until I realized it was God himself who mouth fucked me and raped me. Since then, I have felt weakened and impaired. I was left on the pavement under the rain like the poor festering dead coyote I saw lying on the road next to the 286. I was left forgotten beneath the well, unable to shift or move with my legs and arms ruthlessly strapped and locked together with a prickly cincture cutting circulation around my wrists and ankles. Incapable of speaking or crying out for help. My foul-rotten-decayed tongue lay flat on the wet cobblestone floor in front of my frail crippled scrawny body, as the burgundy, crimson clove-coloured blood that ferally ran from the interior of my mouth to my once inappropriately touched collarbone sinfully christened my tarnished and molested chest.

It is the summer of 1996. It is the last day of July, and it has been the hottest American summer on record since 1974. The cemented pavements and highways of Corpus Christi radiate an extreme and sickening heat, heartlessly melting the tires of its drivers' cars and the soles of its pedestrians' shoes. The grasslands are coarse and dry. The air smells like tangy human sweat and smoke-filled diesel exhaust. Ice cream vans have melted away, and the water from public pools have evaporated into thin air. Cloudless skies and hydrological droughts crack and wrinkle their evangelised citizens' skin. *The cross on top of the mountain* stands highly erected watching this contemporary inferno unfold.

This is my first summer back home from my freshman year at

Arizona State University. The streets of this town and the stringent looks of its inhabitants remind me of who I used to be. The crosses that plague the interior walls of my house remind me of the boy who was once mercilessly burnt alive on the town square for his innocent natural heresies. The priests that nonchalantly walk in the hallways of my family's church boils the blood that streams inside my veins and remind me of the boy who once plotted to behead Father Orlando and dispose of his body by 'El Rio del Rosario' river, but never had the courage to do so. The tacky fluorescent-lit motels in front of the freeways remind me of how the smell of newly clean whitewashed linen exacerbated the olfactory sensory neurons inside my nose when Jimmy used to bury my face on the pillows with his brawny muscular arms whilst he fucked me doggy-style from the back, inside room 301 in 'La Santa Espina' motel. The brown desiccated-leaved forests remind me of the boy who once used to write lustful love stories about two men that would fall in love under a pale blue moonlight in mossy green woodlands in the back of his chemistry notebook when he studied at his desk at night. The musty humid smell inside my room reminds me of the boy who once used to cry at midnight under the covers with a wine bottle shaking on his hand because he feared who he was. *The cross on top of the mountain* that I can see through the window of my room reminds me of my past traumas and troubles, and my undeniable yearning for pure romance and love.

Like a rattlesnake that sheds its old skin on the sands of the desert, this summer, everything was going to change. Maybe the only way I was going to be able to get the golden ticket to heaven was to go through this modern-day hell.

I

Twenty-one

Luke 10:18

He replied,
"I saw Satan fall like lightning from heaven."

Twenty-one trips around the orange scorching sun floating in a trivial insignificant endless vault of darkness. *'Happy twenty-first birthday. Happy birthday to me.'* I quietly mumble to myself, well aware of the fact that I might already be going crazy because it is already too late and there is no good enough reason to stay awake. It is 2AM, 2:39, to be exact. It is the first day of August. Everyone living inside my house is profoundly well asleep. All the lights are off. I sit alone on the cold floor of my room in the dark beneath the golden honey wooden oak cross on my wall. Shirtless, I let the skin of my chest, back and forearms soak in the blue turquoise-hued moonlight that pierces through my window. Unfortunately, there is no pink-frosted 'Tres Leches' cake with any tacky birthday candles to blow out. There is only one unlit candle stuck to the neck of the bottle of a Garganega Pinot Grigio placed next to my two-faced, fraudulent mirror. I have kept this white wine bottle for four years now. This bottle has seen my heart and bones crash, break apart, and then mend in numerous occasions. It has witnessed my deterioration and demise across this perfidious and treacherous town that has destroyed my soul, and sense of self far too many times.

It was the wine bottle Jason and I first shared together, on the midnight of April 22nd, 1992, in the parking lot of Walmart under tall, white, stark lights. Which led to an electrifying make out session and a galvanising mutual oral sex seance. I can still

25

remember tasting the zesty apple, citrus, honeysuckle flavours of the wine when his tongue fought against mine when both of our mouths were tightly interlocked. His girlfriend was Father Orlando's niece, her name was Dolores, and she was bare ugly. He identified as a 'heterosexual', and every time he fucked me, he would blame his sexual and conniving behaviour on the alcoholic volume of the bottle we had drank the night before. He just didn't want to accept that he liked to fuck me and used the nine-dollar Pinot Grigio from Don Gallego's Liquor Store as a mental anaesthetic drug to penetrate me. He used to say, "When you are drunk and horny, a hole is just a hole." But I wanted to be more than just another hole he could fuck whenever he wanted to. I wanted to be his lover. Even if he kept me hidden under the light in secret. That is when my competition with girls commenced and when I started to distrust plain white boring obsolete closeted men.

I get up from the floor, walk across the room, reach for the wine bottle with the candle, and on my way back to the floor I grab the lighter I use to light up my joints. I sit down on the wooden ground and light the candle with my lavender tainted tarot-patterned clipper lighter. The candlelight fills up my room with radiant light, painting the walls with a flickering dancing yellowish orange, egotistically erasing the moonshine that once illuminated my bedroom. I close my eyes firmly. I scrunch up my nose and strongly hold my breath. I nervously clench my hands at the height of my chest and look up at the ceiling.

"Jesus, please take me away from this world," I faintly whisper to myself.

I lack touch and physical affection, so I try to hug myself, folding my arms around my body. But it feels awkward, I am not used to loving myself or used to someone giving me a hug just for the pure sake of it. Most of the hugs I used to get from men would compromise me to end up sleeping with them. Their hugs would always lead to something else, something evil and macabre. One second their muscly veiny arms would be tenderly wrapped around my waist with their chins sweetly tucked in the clavicle near my neck, and the next second, they would be brutally penetrating my body without my consent. I hate to think that over these last twenty-one years of my life, I have let all these ogres and monsters touch my body just because I was sad and horny.

I don't believe Mother when she says she has had no regrets in her life. That is purely not true and humanly possible. Life is full of regrets. We just have a hard time accepting our mistakes and acknowledging the reality that we do in fact regret the decisions we have made in the past. If I could have told my angsty heartbroken fifteen-year-old self to actually kill himself that night after Father Orlando raped me, I *would* have. If I could have told my dazed naive seventeen-year-old self to stop hooking up with Jason in the parking lot of Walmart, I *would* have. If I could have told my four-month-old self fetus living inside my mother's womb to strangle and suffocate himself with the umbilical cord, I *would* have. If I could have told my twenty-year-old self to stop trusting all those two-faced hypocrite souls that he used to call his 'best-friends', I *would* have. If I could have told my nineteen-year-old self to flee away from his hometown far away from the boundaries of his own tradition and religion, I *would* have. If I could have told my thirteen-year-old self to stop sneakily drinking red wine bottles from the cellar in the basement of my house in secret, I *would* have. But *'If'* is only a subordinating conjunction, and a written word. It purely doesn't exist in the quantum physics of the time in our world. Unfortunately, I don't own that magical DeLorean that travels back in time from that science-fiction film I used to watch with Mario and Quique, hidden away from our parents on that VHS tape when I was five, to be able to meticulously alter every little thing that has already happened in my past.

'Twenty-one.' I tardily repeat to myself inside my head in heresy and disbelief as I lose myself in a deep and abstruse trance staring at the wax from the candle drip into the shoulder of the Pinot Grigio bottle. I can now *finally* legally drink alcohol in the United States of America. *'I cannot wait to have my first sip of wine!'* I wish I

could say that with bliss and contentment, but I have been secretly drinking alcohol from the wine bottles my parents kept locked in the cellar in the basement of my house since I was thirteen.

Once when I was twelve, my disquieting and worrying mother caught my sixteen-year-old brother Quique passed out on the dark leather skinned sofa in the basement. The couch that my dogs used to violently scratch, scrape and munch when they were daft and demented puppies. I remember this day with such specific detail. On the Saturday morning of February 19th, 1988, my brother was found with an empty Yellow Tail Shiraz bottle dangling in his quivering left hand. His eyes were deeply shut, and his mouth and chin were smudged with crimson-red stains as if he had just made out with someone in the club with dark cakey burgundy lipstick.

At the stroke of midnight on February 19th, I couldn't fall asleep as I heard Quique vociferously screaming inside his room at 3AM. So, I got out of bed, tiptoed my way out of my bedroom, walked through the cold corridors of the second floor of my house, and stealthily placed my left ear on his wooden oak door, carefully enough to not make any type of noise. I heard him crying. Audibly sobbing. I had never seen or heard my brother crying ever before. He was hyperventilating. And it broke my heart. He was throwing books and objects across the room. I didn't know what was happening. I just remember that he and his vicious cruel Colombian girlfriend had been having lots of problems. And that probably was the night that they had broken up. And from Quique's riotous and topsy-turvy chatter, it looked like she had cheated and broken up with him. Quique was *sixteen* when he first got his heart broken.

After a few moments, I heard him come towards the door, so I quickly sprinted across the hallway and quickly crouched behind the palm-leaved laundry basket that was placed in the middle of the corridor. I saw him dash out of his room, wiping the tears from his blood-shot eyes, and the snot from his running nose. He walked downstairs. I was scared, but then again, fairly intrigued. I meticulously followed him down the staircase.

Suddenly, we had found ourselves in the basement. Near the circumscribed wine cellar. I didn't know what he was doing. I was hiding below the pool table. Trembling. Through the cellar's glass door, I saw him reaching for a wine bottle. He then walked towards the sofa at the other end of the basement and sat on it. He looked towards the white decayed wall in front of him. Tears cascaded down the eyes of his face. He was bizarrely expressionless. He took the top off from the screw cap wine and started mercilessly drinking from it. The scene looked so imposingly beautiful and cinematic. He was just missing a Marlboro cigarette on his lips, haze in the air, and the soft-gauzed black and white filter they used to employ in Old Hollywood noir films in front of him. I was watching the Mexican version of James Dean in Rebel Without a Cause. So, I inherently thought to myself: *'I want to get my heart broken too. I want to run down to the wine cellar one day and dramatically reach for one of those wine bottles. I want to get drunk; cry hysterically and then write about it. I want to feel defeated and make whoever breaks my heart feel worse.'* Although I knew that the situation my brother was going through was his worst-ever nightmare, it was what my dissident twelve-year-old dreams were made of. It felt like whatever had just unfolded in front of my eyes had come directly from a James Stewart movie, and I wanted to be the main protagonist of it. I wanted to feel Quique's emotional pain and wanted God to witness my suffering.

So, a few months later, after my thirteenth birthday on the first of August, I broke my own heart when I realized I had masturbated to the image of Jesus Christ. I broke my own heart when I realized I couldn't ejaculate to the images of the naked women inside Mario's porn magazine hidden on his chest of drawers. I broke my own heart when I realized I didn't want to penetrate a woman with my own homosexual penis, but instead wanted a man to wholeheartedly fuck me. I remember the doom and fright I felt inside my bedroom. *'I am gay.', 'I am a homosexual.'* I remember staring at the ceiling the whole night. My heart was bouncing off my chest. *'What will Mother think?', 'What will Father think?', 'Will they disown me?', 'Am I mentally sick?', 'Am I really a homosexual?', 'Will God send me to hell?', 'Is the world I'm already living in my infernal punishment for being born a homosexual?', 'Is Jesus upset at me now?', 'Did I secretly summon the Devil without knowing?', 'What am I going to do?'* An interrogation light was swinging back and forth above my bed. Scratching my head. Squeezing my brains. Making me sweat until my sheets got exceedingly wet. All these violently brutal questions were moulding me into a cripple, calling me *'God's mistake'*, a walking sin, some wicked man, a burnt creation. They savagely feasted on me, like piranhas devouring me all away. This wasn't the type of heartbreak I had wished upon in the past when I saw my brother drinking his sorrows away with the Yellow Tail Shiraz. This no longer was cinematic, painfully romantic, or beautiful. This was pure barbaric torture. So, there was nothing left to do than doing exactly what my brother did that ill-fated night. I quietly tip-toed out of my room, with tears streaming down my face, and snot dripping from my nose. And at midnight, I promptly walked downstairs to the besieged wine cellar. I looked at the wine cellar and hesitated. I was committing a sin. I was going to get drunk on Jesus's blood. I opened the crystal glass door of the cellar, slowly walked towards a red wine bottle, and nervously reached for the bottle that had the most appealing, enticing, and colourful label. I opened it and devoutly drank from it.

Wine became my best friend. And no one ever knew it. To my parents, I was the young boy who was starting to obey them and rightfully followed the word of God like they had always wanted me to. But deep-down inside, I was broken and thought God had cursed me. So, I started to develop a dark, toxic and twisted relationship with alcohol whenever I would have nightmares in the middle of the night of Mother finding out I was a homosexual and then disowning me. Nightmares of God sending me to hell because I preferred to suck dick instead of eating pussy. Nightmares of getting mutilated and dismembered by God's lightning bolt because of the impure and sinful desires I had of getting penetrated by a man. So, I kept walking down to that wine cellar every night and drank from the narcotic bottles that were able to put me to sleep in an anaesthetic state of mind. Every time Father asked me how I was doing, I lied to his face and said, "Never have been better." But I feared my identity. I feared my sexuality. I was scared of the sexual desires and cravings my body demanded from me. Traumatised by the thought of going to hell and of my family leaving me behind, like a group of lions leaving a cub behind in the desert, dying of thirst on its own. That is when I started to ache, and when my bones started to break. And just like Quique had processed his inexplicable emotions that cataclysmic night with that red wine shiraz, at the age of thirteen, I started to drink my own fears and terrors away in secret every single night. Until one day, Mother brutally locked the wine cellar and started to count the bottles compulsively when she found out that the wine bottles were magically going missing. And as a result, she unjustly grounded Quique for a whole school year because she thought he was the one liable for this happenstance.

II

Umbilical Cord

Isaiah 49:15

*"Can a mother forget the baby at her breast,
and have no compassion on the child she has borne?
Though she may forget,
I will not forget you."*

My name is Antonio Prado Suárez. But I go by *'Tony'*, or at least that is what my white-skinned friends call me by because mouthing the word *'Antonio'* is too lengthy, verbose and Hispanic. I am twenty-one years old, and I was born on August 1st, 1975, in the Christus Spohn Hospital at 6AM. My birth was troublesome, to say the least. I was unfortunately born two months earlier before I was due. I came out of my mother's vagina unexpectedly and uninvited into this dubious and questionable shifting mass of molten rock floating in the middle of a mutinous and anarchical universe after being mercilessly stuck inside my mother's womb for seven months. I was born as an extremely frail and fragile premature baby, and instead of going straight into my mother's arms right after the doctors cut the slimy mucky umbilical cord that superficially connected us, I was sent directly to the Neonatal Intensive Care Unit. I stayed inside a capsulized incubator, all wired and hooked up for two dreary long months. Mother has never said it, but she definitely suffered from postpartum depression after giving birth to me, and that is maybe the reason why she has always felt so disconnected to me.

Throughout my childhood, I felt like an uninvited stranger inside my house. I felt like an outsider, an extra-terrestrial, an outlander. Mother only wanted two children. I was very much

32

unplanned. A remorseful accident. Mother had me when she was thirty-two. Mario and Quique were born five years before that. I was welcomed into this life with repel and regret, and Mother didn't care of hiding that. I sometimes wish she had clandestinely aborted me, but Father and our hypocritical charlatan Catholicism would have never allowed her to do such an '*atrocity*'. She was forced to have me. Maybe that is why she loathed me. Maybe that is why she was unable to breastfeed me. Maybe I was the incarnation of the loss of her autonomy. Maybe I was the curse that was sent to her from the underworld. Maybe I was the consequence of a woman like my mother living under a draconian patriarchal regime. She had every right to be nauseated and repelled by her new-born baby. By me. And no number of bruises or five-year-old tears would be able to forgive God for the absence of a miscarriage. No amount of child-like shame and self-deprecation would be able to forgive Father for murderously denying her own human rights. I know she wanted to abort me, and I only wish she had been given the opportunity and right to do so.

Mario and Quique were the standard I was never able to live up to. They were pretty much invited into this life. Whilst I basically wasn't. Even though Mother didn't expect to have twins, she was happy and content to know that she could get two children out in one push. She always wanted to have two children only, and what better way to have them all at once than having to go through the agonising pain and suffering of each birth. Until, of course, I was unintentionally conceived, and entered this world crudely unwished-for.

Mario and Quique were obedient. Mario and Quique were loving. Mario and Quique did everything Mother told them to do. Mario and Quique fit perfectly into the intricate puzzle of our family. But I didn't. I was the crooked odd old piece that had to squeeze his way into this tyrannical jigsaw. Mother always boorishly compared me to them, and I fucking hated that.

"Ay, Antonio, don't cry! Do you ever see your brothers cry? No! That's because big boys don't cry," she would say screaming

33

at my face when I used to cry because Mario and Quique would unjustly tease me for wanting to go play dress up with my younger female cousin instead of playing soccer with them.

"*Antonio, los vestidos solo son para putas y jotos!* Dresses are only for sluts and faggots!" she would aggressively shake my arms and vociferate at me in the backseat of the car when she buckled me up after I would walk out with Celia, my younger female cousin, in her driveway with a pink ruffled dress on and stubby neon-blue glittery princess-like high heel shoes.

"If only you were more like your brothers, Antonio, you would make me happier, and I would like you more," she would overbearingly bloviate through the rear-view mirror clutching the steering wheel of our navy-blue Ford Caribe with a piercing quality of disappointment and disapproval, whilst I sat on my tightened and measly limited small baby chair in the backseat of the car with tears running down my little innocent cheeks, wishing I could have been more like Mario and Quique. Wishing I could have been more masculine. Wishing I could have held my emotions back as Mario and Quique did. Wishing I could have been more stoic. Wishing I could have made Mother happier. Wishing I could have enticed Mother to love me a little bit more than she actually did. But I always brutishly failed.

The first ever fracture caused on my body was done by Mother when I was only three years old. I can still remember the thunderstruck faces of both Mario and Quique when she snatched the forest emerald, green leathered hardcover '*La Santa Biblia*' and hostilely smacked me on the back of my head with it when I accidentally stubbed my toe on the wooden-oaked table in the hallway and made the '*Virgen de Guadalupe*' ceramic statue that my grandmother bought for Mother's nuptials, drop and shatter all across the floor. There were no boundaries in my household. If you were to make a mistake you were to be punished. Brutally punished. Callously, oppressively, punished. Father never disapproved of her violent and tyrannical manners, and I still hold an abundance of resentment towards him for not standing up for me at any given point in time. His silence contributed to her violence. Almost as if he were being held hostage with handcuffs around his wrists and a tight thread frenziedly sewed between his lips. If Mother was the inquisitor, Father was the accomplice of her bloodthirsty intentions of attempting to eliminate my heresy. They both agreed they were raising us to be strong, substantial men. There was no room for error, weakness or vulnerability. And especially, no room for homosexuality, femininity and sacrilegious blasphemy.

Mother was the owner of the baton inside this house. Everything had to be done the exact way she wanted. If you were to disobey, you had to face her subvert corrupt consequences. She was a powerful, intimidating, fearsome woman. Through my childhood and growing pains, Mother felt more like the evil stepmother from the princess picture books I used to secretly read at my cousin's house than my own actual biological mother. She was big and robust. Her heart was made from wood. Her amber yellow stricken eyes were conceived by baleful reptilian snakes. And the ill-favoured wrinkles of her face exposed the grief and heartbreak her younger self had probably endured.

When I turned six, Mother started to invade my sleepless nights in my dreams. The Wicked Witch of the West looked like a beautiful Greek marble sculpture carved by Aphrodite compared to the sickening putrid foul goblin-like witch version my brain viciously fabricated of Mother in my nightmares. Goblin Witch Mother would stare me down from the corner of my room in the middle of the night. Her shadow and girthy silhouette would encapsulate the entirety of the wooden floorboards. I used to hallucinate that she would sporadically sprint at me with her dislocated and bony limbs with white foam bubbling up from her mouth to her saggy breasts. She would savagely jump on me and would scratch my back with her feisty nails making my spinal veins leak and bleed. She would then brutally puncture my chest with her sharp rusted iron hands piercing right through my frangible stripling ribcage reaching for my crippling beating heart. With my weeping innocent eyes, I would witness my meaty palpitating heart beating on her hand outside of my body. And a blood bath would then stream down from her arm into her legs, making me bleed until my merciless death. I would scream out of fright and pain, and she would primitively munch on my heart like a coyote that hadn't feasted on poor little lambs for more than two weeks. As a child, this was what my violent and hellish nightmares were made of. And Mother was coincidentally and unsurprisingly always the barbarian, monstrous, protagonist of them.

Starvation has always been something my body has been accustomed to. The first time I was forced to starve myself was when I was fourteen years old, and Mother locked me in the cupboard of our basement for twelve hours straight as punishment for finding a hidden heterosexual porn magazine under my bed that I secretly and covertly stole from Mario's chest of drawers. I remember the darkness that encapsulated my whole gaze and the smell of mould that brutishly impregnated my lungs. The sad sombre light that shone through the crack of the tyrannical locked door obliged me to look at the cross of Jesus on the wall in front of me for an endless spiral of time. I screamed and thumped, and begged for forgiveness, but no one inside the household came downstairs to unlock the door. Not Mario. Not Quique. Not Father. No one. Everyone was an accomplice of Mother's cruel and vicious abuses. They were the bystander tourists inside their own safe caged truck in a South African safari watching the predator eat their prey alive. After a few hours, there was nothing left to do, but to pray. So, I knelt down on my knees, clenched my shaking hands together and prayed for mercy and pitiless clemency. I pounded my forehead back and forth on the caramel-oaked wooden panels of the wall swearing to myself I would *burn* that magazine full of men grandiloquently penetrating vaginas with their own erected penises. I pledged and vowed, and stipulated before Jesus that I would never touch myself down there ever again.

My stomach loudly gurgled and rumbled. My digestive system had only digested my saliva and the proteolytic enzymes of my small intestine in the past pitiful long-drawn-out twelve hours. There were no red wine bottles to drink to distract myself either. I was to face my own sins locked in a dark room all the way down in the basement of my house without any food or water. Although I was only there for twelve hours, there was no way on earth Mother would have left me rotting down there for more than twenty-four hours. So, at the end of the day, it was just a game of patience, and getting accustomed to what it felt like to starve to death. Hunched up in the corner of the cupboard, with my arms behind my head and my face engrossed between both of my legs, I wept and cried out of shame, anger, humiliation and hunger. The salty tears that streamed down my cheeks inundated the entirety of the cold grey cemented floor. The murky snot from my nose sledged into the hair follicles of my newly grown teenage hairy legs. My wet warm pants and the piss puddles on the ground gave the interior of the cupboard a pungent and peppery smell. And the cross of Jesus that hung on the wall above my head looked down upon me viciously. Gruelling me for my lustful sinful desires.

After a few hours of staring at the ants walking back and forth on the floor I heard some footsteps coming downstairs. Holy fuck. *'I hope that is Mother.'* Through the threshold of the door, I saw a big, tall silhouette covering the synthetic artificial light coming from upstairs. It was in fact Mother. *'Thank fuck.'* I heard some keys rustling and dangling from her pocket into the lock of the doorway. She unlocked the door. I looked up at her like an inmate in death row waiting for the day and time of his execution. She opened the door wide open with no pity on her face and coldly walked away like a white ruthless republican police officer. Light came inside the claustrophobic room like the bright orange-hued light a servant sees when their master opens the rustic wooden iron door of their dungeon in the morning. I slowly stood up. My denim jeans were humid and stale, drenched in my own urine. I dusted myself off and tiptoed my way out of the cupboard.

After that day and incident, I was mortally scared of seeing

37

Mother or anyone else inside my household. Mother knew I was different. Mother was spooked about the fact that I had sexual desires, but most significantly, she was petrified by the intrusive thought that I might have been born a homosexual, and that in turn our family had been cursed by the Devil. So, she avoided talking to me at all costs and ordered Father to move my bedroom to the third floor of the house which initially served as the attic. Mother wanted to limit physical interaction between me and my family as much as possible. Mother wanted to contain and incarcerate the demons that had already possessed me. So, she exiled me to the third floor of the house where no one else lived to avoid and prevent a satanic and diabolical contagion from spreading within the household.

III

Jimmy

1 Corinthians 6:13

"You say, 'Food for the stomach and the stomach for food,
and God will destroy them both.'
The body, however,
is not meant for sexual immorality but for the Lord,
and the Lord for the body."

Jimmy was a white American. He was tall and hench. He had piercing blue eyes. He was the embodiment of what Aryan dreams were made of. His hair was long and luscious with blonde and reddish tints, with each strand of hair ardently flaming into fire. Although his silhouette was industrially masculine, his doll-like nose gave him a quality of femininity and susceptibility. His lips were coarse and dry, but plump and juicy, wet enough to sensually brush my spinal cords with the brims of his muzzle. His chargrilled breath on my skin would warm up the entirety of my body in the snap of a finger. His prickly stubble would make my chin bleed after a big, long kiss and would leave red purple rashes underneath my hips. He had a brown mole on his left cheek, and had freckles sprinkled all the way from the back of his neck to his lower back. His arms were strong and veiny, reminiscent of the swollen hormone-injected chicken thighs you find in the supermarket. His hands were erotic and feisty. They were perfect for slapping my ass cheeks violently. And his penis was big and monumental.

Jimmy said he didn't like boys. He used to say he wasn't a homosexual. And that was the reason why I fell in love with him. But I was the exception. I became the only male in his life he was

39

willing to fuck. And maybe that was because I was naive and gullible.

I met Jimmy outside the 'Hope and Anchor' bar two blocks away from San Padre Island Drive Frontage Road at the dead of night. I was young, newly eighteen, and horny. I would sometimes get out of the house in the middle of the night to try to find men near bars I could cruise with. I needed to feel loved. I yearned to be held. But most importantly, I needed the male validation I was never able to obtain.

The 'Hope and Anchor' bar was not a bar that gay men would go to at night, but it most certainly had the men I was attracted to. The rugged, masculine, hairy men that flooded all of my wet dreams. And, as I had previously experienced in the past, when creepy lustful men are drunk, a hole is just a hole. Whether it'd be a female hole or a male hole. It wouldn't matter. They would fuck it regardless until it would satisfy their needs. And frankly, I didn't mind undermining myself. I just wanted to be a hole where men could brutally drill their dicks inside. I wanted to feel desired. I wanted to feel wild and go against everything everyone had ever advised me not to do. I wanted to feel like I was doing something dangerous. I wanted to feel like I was eating the forbidden fruit in The Garden of Eden.

Jimmy looked sober and tranquil when he walked out of the bar when the clock hit two. He was alone. He walked towards his bronze, brown pick-up Chevy truck parked in the sketchy dusty parking lot and jumped onto the bonnet of his car. He was wearing a white ribbed tank top with faded blue bootcut Levi's jeans. He had a beautiful western buckle belt on that sat tightly above his denim bulge. I could already tell he had a huge dick. His skin was golden tan, adorned with blonde, yellow hair foliage. He had a Realtree Camo baseball cap that scooped his heavenly blonde-ginger locks. His dangling big feet were decorated with chunky black-leather boots with a stocky silver buckle that tied the whole shoe together at the ankle. His beard was unclean and unkempt. Just how I liked my men. It looked like he hadn't showered in a few days, and that intrinsically turned me on. I could smell his manly and red-blooded sweat from the front of the Chevy truck where he was sitting, all the way to the alleyway where I was secretly hiding.

Jimmy took out a pack of blonde infused Lucky Strikes out of his pocket. This was my chance. I was going to have to do the classic thing everybody does when they want to have a flirt, and go ask him for a cigarette. But from the looks of it, he looked like one of those men that hated homosexuals. But I, thankfully, didn't look like one. So, I took a deep breath in and out. I rustled my curly thick hair with my hands and decided to tiptoe my way to him. I walked across the parking lot. Big, tall streetlights exposed my overwrought silhouette. My heart was beating fast, my hands were trembling, and I could feel the kick-off of an erection piercing through my underwear. My mouth was getting drier and drier, and I just wanted to run the other way, but I promised myself that I had to keep going.

He was sat there motionlessly. He was smoking his cigarette, slowly dangling his legs in the air, directly looking at the entrance of the bar, watching the drunk and inebriated people walk out of the bar. I clenched my fists, bit my lips and steeled myself. I approached him.

"Can I have a cigarette?" I coyly uttered, soundlessly interrupting his solitude and serenity.

He looked up at me and without even thinking about it said "Yes."

He gently handed me the pack. "Thanks," I quietly asserted.

I took out a cigarette and placed it on my lips.

"Here ya go," he handed me his neon yellow lighter.

I lit up my cigarette and slowly gave it a hit. He quietly smoked and so did I. Silence consumed us. We were both mute and tense. Hushed and wordless, he didn't mutter a single word. *'Fuck. What do I do now?'* I thought to myself. *'Is he waiting for me to leave?', 'Yeah, he definitely is waiting for me to leave.'* I awkwardly stood in front of his car not knowing what to do, trying to observe the drunk people that were coming out of the bar. But I was too nervous to even think or process what was unfolding before my eyes.

"Do you wanna come up?" he gently gestured.

"Yeah sure," I attempted to climb on top of the tall front part of the Chevy but was unable to do so. *'Fuck. Fuck. Fuck. Come on Tony, play it cool.'* My limbs were weak, I struggled to ascend.

"Let me give you a hand," he grabbed me by the arm and lifted me up. His hands were clammy and sweaty.

"Ah, thank you," I sighed. He touched me and it felt like a kiss on the neck. *'Fuck me already.'* I could feel cupid's arrow perforating my heart. I tried to find a comfortable position next to him. We both sat down on the front part of his pick-up truck, observing our surroundings.

"What is a boy like you doing around here at these hours?" he clumsily asked, taking a puff from his Lucky strike.

"I was unable to sleep."

He raised his eyebrow. "So, you came here…?" He was trying to find a reason why a boy who was unable to sleep decided to walk all the way outside from his house to the exterior of a bar full of drunk truck drivers and trailer trash men, who were trying to hide away from their wives.

"Yeah… I was bored, and was craving a cigarette—"

"How old are you?" he quickly interrupted me.

"Eighteen," I forcefully smiled and clenched my teeth nervously.

He chuckled.

"What?" I suddenly felt ashamed and self-conscious.

"Nothing," he tenderly smiled at me.

"How old are *you*?"

He cackled even louder. Smoke came out from his nostrils.

Jimmy gazed deeply into the pupils of my eyes. Out of nowhere, he had broken the barrier and wall between us. The ice had already been broken. "You don't want to know."

I looked up at him puzzled and perplexed. I didn't know what to say.

"I'm 32," he firmly stated.

"Oh, you are not *that old.*"

"14 years older than *you.*"

"Well—"

"Why are you here?" he abruptly interrupted me, raising his left eyebrow even higher than before.

"As I said, I was unable to sleep—"

"No, no, why are you *really* here?" he cunningly smirked at me.

I nervously laughed and threw my arms into the air. We both looked at each other's eyes deeply. The strain and tension between each other was getting stronger and stronger. We were both irresponsibly pulling on a rubber band that was about to break.

"Do you wanna go take a ride in this car?" he said with his gentle, charming, Eastern Virginia accent.

"Yeah, why not," I shyly answered.

I knew that he knew what I wanted. And that was exciting.

We both looked at each other's eyes, knowing deep down inside that we were both about to play with fire. But if we were to get burnt in the end, at least we would have already been electrified first.

Jimmy parked us right in front of the North Padre Seawall. By that time, it was already about 4:30AM. The windows of the Chevy were frosted with our humid breath and unchaste sweat.

Jimmy was on top of me and shirtless, restraining my arms and hands on top of my long-haired head. He brutishly kissed me. He grunted in my ears with each kiss he gave me on the neck, whilst I scratched his white pale back with fervour and immoral vehemence. Our lips were tightly intertwined, exchanging each other's oxygen and carbon dioxide fumes. He tasted like Budweiser and tobacco, which beautifully exacerbated my taste buds. The fiery stubble on his chin scraped the skin of my sweet innocent cheeks which made my eyes roll back like a demonically possessed child. The way he slowly thrusted his bulge underneath his faded blue Levi's into my lower abdomen made me want to bite his lips right off. So, I bit a part of his cheeks. My lustful tongue savoured the sweat from his bristled beard. I set him apart for a second and held the back of his head tightly. His aggressive volatile reptilian eyes looked right into me.

"Choke me," I desperately whimpered.

He gripped my neck with his meaty Aryan monster-ogre hands firmly. He tightly squeezed the trachea of my neck with his corpulent fingers, making sure no oxygen would pass through my windpipe. I tried to breathe. But I couldn't. I liked that feeling and conniving sensation of not knowing when to scream 'Stop!'

"Harder!" I muttered.

He choked me harder and interlocked his hands between my neck even more ferociously than before. I loudly moaned. But then suddenly, I remembered that I wasn't back home, and I had to be back home before sunrise and before Mother would wake up. If Mother were ever to find out that I sneakily fled out of the house in the middle of the night my whole life would have already been over. Through the suffocation and lack of air, I saw these gritty and graphic consequences flash past my eyes. My heart started to beat faster and faster. This sexual encounter had to unfortunately come to an end in a matter of two hours. So, I grabbed his hands away from my neck and signalled him to stop. He stopped. I could see the concern on his face, worried that maybe he had gone too far.

"I have to be back by sunrise," I hesitantly said.

"What time is it?" he quickly looked at his tacky golden metal digital Casio watch, "It's 5:20!"

"Okay, it's not that late, but I have to be back as soon as possible," I nervously stuttered.

"Don't worry, I'll drive you back."

"Are you sure?"

"Yes."

"Do you promise?"

"Yes," he gently kissed me on the lips.

"Okay," I smiled.

"But let me fuck you first," he took hold of my waist tightly.

"Fuck me hard," I bit my lower lip and tried to act like his little dirty slut.

He brusquely dashed his western buckle belt off. He belligerently took his denim bootcuts off, followed by his white creamed Calvin Kleins. Like an aggressive elephant trunk, his long-awaited pink veiny blushed throbbing penis catapulted from his jock cup into the air.

The 27th of October 1993 was the day we both lit each other's matches. I thought I would never see Jimmy ever again in my life but before he dropped me at the driveway of my house at 6:40AM, he took a pen and a wrinkled receipt paper from his pocket and wrote his telephone number on the back of it.

"Here's my number if you need anything," he murmured, "I'll see you next Thursday at 'La Santa Espina' Motel at 12AM sharp in room 301," he tucked my long hair behind my ears.

"Okay," I looked down at the paper and then looked up at him and smiled. *This can't be real'* I thought to myself. *'A man likes me!', 'A man **loves** me!'* Ants childishly danced up my spine, and butterflies buoyantly flapped their wings against the interior walls of my stomach.

Mwah. He kissed me goodbye.

I slowly opened the wooden front door of my house and stealthily walked all the way to the third floor, into my room. Thankfully, everybody was still asleep. But most importantly, Mother. When I got into my bedroom, I furtively slammed the door shut. I quickly took my jeans and T-shirt off and dived into the cotton covers of my bed in my underwear. I hugged my pillows tightly and joyfully laughed. I felt ecstatic and happy. I felt loved. A feeling I had never felt in my life ever before. Rays of sunlight started to peek through the shutters of my window. *'You've made it home by sunrise.'* I sighed.

Lost in my thoughts, I looked up at the ceiling and tried to close my eyes. But the ants and butterflies inside my body kept me wide awake.

$$***$$

It was the hot scorching night of the 4th of November 1993. Seven days after Jimmy and I had first met at the 'Hope and Anchor'. It was 2:32AM and I was in room 301 at 'La Santa Espina' motel, situated in the intersection between the 286 and the 358. The white plastic cheap ceiling fan kept spinning rapidly above my sweaty naked body, which lounged on the mattress that had been used by many other prostitutes and horny fifty-year old men to fornicate behind closed doors, hidden away from their spouses. The dazzling, yellow, fluorescent lights coming from the washroom where Jimmy was wiping the semen off his pulsating penis with coarse linen toilet roll after he had ejaculated inside of me a few moments before, filled every little corner of the darkened-room space.

Jimmy formerly originated from the Eastern Shore of Virginia but moved to Corpus Christi ten years ago after he got promoted into a higher role in the truck hiring company he worked for. His wife and children lived in Virginia, and he went to visit them every three months. He used to say he wasn't fond of homosexuality or homosexuals, but he liked the way I would let him touch me. He said that his wife's hairy vagina had dried and loosened up after giving birth to his twin boys, Bryce and Carter. He said he fancied my athletic, muscular, youthful masculine physique. He liked the fact that I was young, wild and eighteen. He loved the tightness around the opening of my rectum. And I loved his stout-hearted American penis.

Jimmy and I spent that whole night staring at the ceiling fan in unison. We talked about his life, before we had both lost track of time and he had to drive me back home before sunrise. He told me stories about how he used to drive all across the country. My face rested on his ginger-hairy swollen chest, and his stocky fingers traced my bushy thick darkened eyebrows. This man had lived. He had endured pain and hardship. He had been jailed and emancipated, but he still wanted to spend an evening talking to an eighteen-year-old who had barely lived anything in his life yet. Jimmy was an enigma I wanted to decrypt. And I had a lot of questions that needed answers.

"Where do you live?" I confidently asked.

"I live here, in Corpus Christi," he quickly asserted.

"How come you are staying in this motel then?"

"Oh, this is just where I take people like you."

'Oh.', 'What did he mean by 'people like you'?', 'Was I just another sneaky lover?', 'Was I just another hookup?', 'Was I playing the role of his closeted and unlabelled prostitute?', 'Wasn't I as special as I thought?' My mind started to spiral out of control. "What do you mean?" I overbearingly asked.

"I feel more comfortable bringing people here."

"So, are you seeing other people?" I could feel the jealousy boiling in the blood of my veins.

"Not now, no. It's just you… I guess… At the moment," he childishly giggled, "and my wife…"

"Okay…"

"What?"

"Nothing… I was just curious."

"I like you," he touched my cheek with his warm sweaty hand, "a lot."

"Me too."

"There's something about you—"

"I wish you could show me where you lived," I sharply interrupted.

"Don't get ahead of yourself, Tony. Let's keep it here for now."

"But I want to see your house…"

"Shhh…" he shushed me with a kiss on the lips and rapidly moved on top of me. Our tongues slowly swayed and danced conjointly. I squeezed his hand tightly in mine. He bellicosely thrusted his pelvic area on me. This was more than just a hookup. This no was longer a game. We had broken all of our unspoken and tongueless rules. The wood started to burn, and our bones started to melt. We were no longer playing with fire; both of our bodies had already started to burn to death.

***

Jimmy never referred to me as his boyfriend or his 'lover'. To him, I was just his fourteen years younger, eighteen-year-old friend. A fourteen years younger, eighteen-year-old friend that would suck his dick for an endless amount of time. A fourteen years younger, eighteen-year-old friend that would spread his ass cheeks wide open whenever he would snap his fingers. Yes. I was bitter for just being his *fourteen years younger, eighteen-year-old friend'*. And I used to roll my eyes every time he would foolishly bloviate those words out of his mouth. But I was too naive to think that he was ever going to call me his boyfriend or lover. He was fourteen years older than me. And he was probably extremely ashamed that he liked to fuck me. But if I was his age, I would have probably felt ashamed too. I never took the time to analyse the psychology behind his actions. The most important thing to me was that someone out of nowhere had suddenly found interest in me. In a time where I felt unloved and underappreciated by Mother and Father, by Mario and Quique, by my friends, God, Jesus, and by my life, Jimmy's sexual attraction towards me was the thing I held onto the most. It was the thing that kept me going. It was the thing that gave me purpose in life. It was the thing that kept me on my feet. And it was the thing that kept me alive.

Jimmy and I kept seeing each other in secret in 'La Santa Espina' motel every Thursday. It quickly became our weekly ritual. Mother had her suspicions, but she hardly ever heard me sneaking out of the house every time I clandestinely left. I was really good at keeping secrets. I had been keeping lots of secrets locked all the way in the vault of my own traumatised brain all my life. My friend Charlotte used to say that there was only one rule when having a friend with benefits, and that was to not catch feelings whatsoever. But how the fuck do you not catch feelings for a man that keeps inserting his penis inside of you every week? I was stupid and eighteen. Jimmy, to me, was my confidante, my companion, the person who knew most of my deepest secrets, the person I had ever loved the most in that point of my life. Jimmy, to me, was more than just a bulky piece of meat or body. Jimmy was the person I had been waiting for my entire life. But I was delusional. And delusion became my best friend. I thought that the man that was fourteen years older than me and that held my waist tightly in a special sort of way was destined to become the love of my life. But to him, I *was* the piece of meat he got to play with every Thursday. To him, I was just a dumb child he could play mind tricks on. To him, I was a sex toy with no feelings. I was just a disposable wooden toy he could toss in the highway whenever he would finally get bored. To him, I was just someone he could fuck. He never cared about what I had to say. He never cared about the situations that had traumatised me in

49

the past. He only liked to speak about himself and how he wanted to endlessly fuck and destroy me. And, although that was flattering to hear, I wanted him to love me, not to lustfully desire me.

I remember coming back home crying every Friday morning because I didn't want to accept the fact that he didn't love me. I remember looking at myself deeply in the mirror. I would caress my chest and ribs and wet my wooden floorboard with my tears. *'If he liked to fuck me, why didn't he love me?'* I started to feel the neglect and the rejection. The dismissal and abandonment I had felt my whole entire life.

Jimmy wasn't the person I had created in my own mind. Jimmy was just Jimmy. And even though he only thought about me minutes before our weekly fucking session, he lived rent-free in my mind from morning to night every day of the week. He was the first person I thought about waking up and the last person I would think about before going to sleep. It was unfair and unjust. *'Why the fuck had I decided to sneak out of my house that midnight when I was desperately looking for a man to fuck in the 'Hope and Anchor'?', 'Why the fuck did I ask him for that blonde infused Lucky Strike?', 'Why the fuck did I let him fuck me in the first place?'* Self-hatred and unanswerable questions started to consume my nights and days. I began to lose my appetite. I would go up to my parents' bathroom every morning to weigh myself on the scale and that is when I decided to start starving myself again. My heart was heavy, but my bones were brittle and weak. If we had both decided to play with fire in the beginning, why was I the only one burning alive? Maybe he knew all along that he was going to be the inquisitor and I was going to be the witch he could sinfully incinerate to death. Maybe there was something even more sinister lurking underneath the surface. Maybe he saw and smelled my susceptibility and vulnerability all along and took advantage of it. Maybe he knew that I needed some sort of saviour, and he needed someone to uplift him and worship him like a Messiah.

***

It was the 24th of December 1993. Only about a month and three weeks had passed since I first met Jimmy. But it felt like I had met him more than a year ago. It felt like I had been carrying the weight he had placed on my shoulders for more than a lifetime. It felt like he had left a punctured dagger in the right side of my lower back for more than a century. My rusted and oxidised blood clogged the arteries of my heart.

Christmas was a time to be jolly and happy. But I have never liked Christmas. I have always found it to be the most depressing holiday of the year. It was the only time in the year where I was unfortunately forced to spend time with my family. Mother would incarcerate and jail us inside the household for the entirety of the holiday period. We never really got presents like all the other children. Santa Claus never delivered presents to our family in Christmas morning. Mother never supported those types of heresies and magical entities. According to Mother, Christmas was meant to celebrate the birth of Jesus, and everything else was irrelevant and unimportant. Mother was devoted to Jesus and to God. And Christmas was the time she would force that type of worship and devotion to us the most. It was the time to go to church with all the family for an endless amount of time and praise our Lord Jesus Christ.

That year, Christmas Eve fell on a Thursday. The day Jimmy and I had agreed on to see each other every week since the beginning of November. However, this time, Jimmy told me to meet him in front of *the cross on top of the mountain* at 12AM instead of 'La Santa Espina' motel. The only problem was that in a Mexican household Christmas is celebrated on the 24th of December. The festivities would usually start at 8PM and would commonly finish around 4AM on the 25th. But this was the last time I was going to be able to see Jimmy in a long while as he was going to be driving upstate to Virginia the next day to visit his wife and children. The stakes were high, and my eighteen-year-old-self did not know how to cope with these high levels of

51

stress and adrenaline. This was Mother's favourite day of the year, and there was no way I could possibly ruin it for her. I had to come up with a solution as fast as possible. *'How was I going to potentially excuse myself from this celebration, especially on Christmas Eve?'* This was going to be impossible.

I was nervous throughout the whole evening. Unable to eat or speak a word. All my family members gathered up around the dinner table and loudly laughed as they talked to each other. But I felt distant to all that buzz and chatter. My eyes were on the clock, and my head was on Jimmy. I did not want to be there with my family, and I did not want to celebrate the birth of Jesus. I left the turkey bathed in gravy and mashed potato untouched. I was so stressed and worked-up that if I were to eat, I would have vomited right away. Mother glanced at me across the table. She could tell something was off. She could tell something was wrong. But she never had the emotional intelligence, or affection to ever ask me if I was okay. She tried to ignore my uncomfortable and depressing aura, and without a hitch, tried to enjoy the holiday she had been waiting all year long to celebrate with the rest of her family.

It was 11:30PM and I had to be on *the cross on top of the mountain* in thirty minutes. But my family was still on the dining table savouring their Christmas Eve dried fruit cake. My uncles and cousins kept talking loudly to one another. Mother looked content and happy, and glamorously cackled with Mario and Father. My heart was beating out of my chest. This had to be the worst Christmas I had ever experienced in my life. I had to leave now. I had to *go* see Jimmy. But what was I going to say? Then it all hit me, like a brick on the head. This was going to be unfeasible. I was going to have to wait until later in the night to go to *the cross on top of the mountain*, when everyone had already gone to sleep, hoping that Jimmy would still wait for me until I showed up. So, I took a deep breath in and out and tried to enjoy the moment. I tried to convince myself that it was all going to work out, and it was all going to be alright. I tried to assure myself that he was going to be waiting for me until I appeared.

On a few occasions in the past, I had run a few hours late for our weekly fucking sessions, and he would wait for me inside the room of the motel until I emerged. So, there wasn't really any reason to worry about anything. The only peculiar thing was that he wanted to meet at *the cross on top of the mountain* instead of the motel like we always did. But maybe he just wanted a change of scenery. Maybe we were going to fuck inside his car with the view of the city at night. Or maybe he just wanted to surprise me with something. I didn't know. All I knew is that I wanted all my family members go from my house as soon as possible so I could go see Jimmy.

It was 2:30AM. My aunts, uncles and older cousins, had been drinking since 8PM, as well as my brothers and parents. They were all starting to get drunk and tired. Tia Laura was already falling asleep on the sofa, and Tio Pepe had his head resting on the table. I could envision this Christmas Eve celebration finally coming to an end. After a few moments, my family members started to greet each other goodbye, and Mother quite drunkenly and inebriated walked our family guests outside the house. Intoxicated people started to leave one after the other until only Mother, Father, Mario, Quique and I were the only people left inside the living room.

"I'll pick up everything tomorrow morning — I'm too tired now," Mother said in an intoxicated manner, stumbling on her words.

"Don't worry, I'll help you tomorrow morning," I excitedly stated. Trying to keep my feet from going out the front door.

"Thank you," she coldly and deeply looked into my eyes.

'Oh shit. What is she going to say now?'

"Goodnight, Antonio."

"Goodnight, Mother."

Mother and Father slowly walked towards their bedroom next

to the living room. Mario and Quique walked upstairs to their room. I stayed downstairs and started to clear plates from the dining room into the kitchen. After twenty minutes or so, I decided I had to go. It was 3:20AM and it would have taken me about 30 minutes to walk all the way up to *the cross on top of the mountain.*

'I could actually make this happen.', 'I could actually make it there for 4AM sharp.', 'I hope Jimmy is still horny enough to wait for me there!'

Out of breath, I finally arrived at the top of the mountain. I saw the big iron *cross* in the distance and saw a brown, bronze Chevy pick-up truck parked right next to it. *'Fuck yeah!', 'He is still there!', 'He waited for me!', 'He is definitely horny!', 'He is going to fuck the living brains out of me!'* So, without any hesitation, I ran as fast as I could to the car. Enough time had passed already, and I didn't want to waste any other minute.

I arrived in front of the car and saw the driver's seat door open. The headlights were still on. The radio inside the car was playing loud Rockabilly music from cool oldies 96 FM. The engine was on with the car brake. But where was Jimmy? *'Was this some sort of prank?'* I was scared. I went inside the car to try to look for answers. There was a pink lube bottle lying and leaking on the car floor. A pair of sunglasses laid on top of the passenger's seat. The glove box was open, but there was nothing there. I got outside the car and checked my surroundings. But there was no one there. I could only hear the owls or the harmless wildlife animals rustling behind the leaves of the trees of the mountain. I stumbled upon two Jack Daniel's bottles on the coarse and dried-out grass, they were probably Jimmy's. I picked up one whiskey bottle and threw it across the distance. I was trying to catch someone's attention.

"JIMMYYYYY!" I screamed into the air.

No answer.

"JIMMYYYYY!" I howled once again. But this time my voice

cracked towards the end of the scream.

No answer.

Suddenly, my heart started to feel really heavy. Something was off. Something had gone terribly wrong. I could feel it all across my chest. The Devil was gleaming down upon me. I could sense him. Anxiety started to consume my whole body. I started to scratch my face out of dread and fear.

"JIMMYYYYYY, PLEASEEEE!" I cried out.

No answer, once again. An owl hooted. But no one else answered.

'Fuck! Where the fuck is he!?'

In that split second, I saw some footsteps on the muddy floor. They were Jimmy's footsteps. They were reminiscent and of the same size as his big black leather motorcycle boots. But I didn't like where this was going. I could feel a dark shadow hanging on the right side of my shoulder. I was hyperventilating, clenching my fists tightly. The air was getting colder and colder on top of the mountain. Vapour and haze came out of my mouth.

I slowly started to follow the footsteps. But they were all leading to somewhere I didn't want to go. The footsteps were leading all the way to the cliff of the mountain. *'No. This can't be real.'* So, I kept walking on top of Jimmy's footsteps. They leaded me all the way to the end of the cliff. Tears started to brutishly fall from the corners of my eyes onto the dirtied floor. Blood started to stream slower and slower through my veins. My hearing was getting worse and worse. My ears were ringing out loud. The grim reaper was holding my neck tightly.

I arrived at the end of the cliff and closed my eyes. I clenched my hands at the height of my chest. I tried not to lean too forward to not fall into the void. After a few seconds, I tried to find some sort of braveness and gallantry inside of me and opened my eyes. I slowly swallowed my saliva and looked down into the abyss.

I had never experienced that type of physical pain and terror in my life ever before. My heart stopped beating for a few seconds. My mouth dropped wide open all the way down to the bottomless pit. I squealed and quickly put my hands over my mouth. *'This has to be a nightmare, this has to be a nightmare.'*

Jimmy's dead body rested all the way down on the highway below the cliff. And it looked like a few cars had already passed over his rotten putrid corpse. Sombre yellow tall highway lights exposed every little grotesque detail of his mutilated remains. I had never seen that type of gore and violence ever before in my life. This was sanguinary and slaughterous porn. Jimmy had killed himself. *'Why?'* Jimmy had a wife and two children waiting for him in Virginia for Christmas day. *'Why did he do this?', 'Why did he want to meet at the cross on top of the mountain instead of the motel?', 'Did he want me to see how he would kill himself?', 'What if someone actually pushed him and it wasn't him?'* Questions were running past my brain at 300 miles per hour. I didn't know what to do. I put my hands on my face and I boisterously cried. I was unable to move. Like a vegetable, I froze into a static position. But I had to run. I had to go. So, I looked down at his dismembered corpse lying on the highway once again, paid my respects, said goodbye, and quickly ran away.

I got to my house around 6AM. I undressed myself bare naked and threw myself into my bed. I buried my face into the pillow and lavishly cried, making sure no one would be able to hear me. *'How was this possible?', 'How is this even real?', 'How am I ever going to move on from this?', 'How did God and Jesus allow Jimmy to do this?', 'Jimmy was going to rot in hell.', 'Suicide was the worst of sins you could ever commit in God's realm.'* I looked up at the ceiling coldly. Tears streamed down the sides of my cheeks onto the pillows. Thoughts and questions kept racing inside my mind, keeping me wide awake, crudely torturing me. My chest felt tight and oppressively stiff. It felt harder and harder to breathe, as time passed by.

The sun started to rise outside my window.

"Merry Christmas," I murmured to myself, whilst I still wept and cried. So, I grabbed the pillow beside me and rested my face on it the same way I used to rest my head on Jimmy's ginger-hairy chest.

IV

The Texan Drive In

Genesis 6: 11-12

*"Now the earth was corrupt in God's sight
and was full of violence.
God saw how corrupt the earth had become,
for all the people on earth had corrupted their ways."*

It is the day after my 21st birthday; the second of August 1996. It has been a very mundane and monotonous summer so far. There isn't much to do here. However, I do like to go for long walks in the neighbourhood or grab Mario's car and drive to Lucio's Pizzeria and get a classic diavola pizza. I like to watch the cars pass by on the highway whilst I eat my pizza on the opened trunk of my SUV at the parking lot. Apart from greasy pepperoni American pizzas and scorching, anxiety-inducing long walks, I have also taken myself to the Alamo Drafthouse Cinema where I watch horror films on my own. I recently watched Amityville Dollhouse. It was pure shit. But my friend Marcia works there, and she always lets me sneak into any of the screenings I want to see. She is the junior supervisor of the cinema, and when I go there, she spoils me with free popcorn and nachos.

This July, I had a creative epiphany where I discovered I wanted to become a writer in the future. So, I started to write a lot. Most of the days since I have been back home, I've stayed inside my room writing about my life and my past. Coming back from Arizona State for the summer has been overwhelming and confounding. I have discovered a lot of things about myself that I wasn't aware of, which has also brought a lot of stuff from the past back to the surface. Stuff I have been trying to supress my entire life. Leaving home and Corpus Christi for college allowed me to repress all the heavy experiences I had endured in this town. But supressing stuff never works, because the past will always weave its way into the present no matter how much you try to repress it. I knew that coming back home from college for the summer was going to unleash all these clandestine demons once again. And like a Devil that never dies, these emotions and experiences from the past kept lurking back to the surface.

This afternoon I decided to take myself on a drive to 'The Texan Drive In'. I wanted to get my first official legal drink at the bar as a celebration of my 21st birthday. I didn't tell anyone, nor did I invite any of my friends. I wanted to go by myself. I wanted to sit down, have a drink and relax as much as I could, to carefully observe the customers inside the bar. I had a thunderstorm striking inside my mind and I wasn't really in the mood to speak to anyone. I was feeling reflective. But I also felt lost and confused. Turning twenty-one yesterday, made me realise that I have nothing figured out. It made me realise that I have no clue of what I want to do with my life. I feel lonely and desolate. I only have two real friends in my life. And my parents barely talk to me. And although the Texan sun shines brightly all day long, I wish it didn't because it forces me to feel happy when I'm truly not.

No one in my life knows I'm a homosexual. Marcia and the guys I've fucked back in college are the only exception. I feel alienated and estranged. No one in my life likes to make me feel special anymore. No one said 'Happy Birthday' to me. Not even Mother. The only gift I got was a cheap one-dollar hallmark birthday postcard that Father left on the kitchen counter the next morning. That was it. No one else put more effort into showing their love and affection towards me. I sometimes feel like everybody hates me. Because if they actually didn't, I probably would have received way more birthday wishes and presents than the actual tacky generic gas station store postcard Father gave me.

"Can I have a Budweiser on tap please?" I politely asked the bartender.

"ID please," she rudely answered with a chewing gum in her mouth. She was voluptuous and masculine. I couldn't tell whether she was a man or a woman. Her voice was harsh and unrefined. She wasn't a pretty person to look at. She had a messy ponytail and a big octopus tattoo plastered on her right saggy shoulder. Her eyes were embellished with tacky blue eye shadow. Her fat and voluminous upper body was draped with a tight and extra-small unwashed black crop top.

"Here," I handed her my ID from my wallet. She snapped it out of my fingers aggressively and looked at it closely making sure I wasn't deceiving her.

"You just turned 21 then," she sarcastically cackled.

"Yeah, yesterday."

She rapidly moved to the bar taps and poured a Budweiser with her fatty glutinous arms.

"Here ya go, faggot!" she savagely slammed the glass on the bar counter and forcefully smiled at me, "5.50, please."

"Thanks," I smiled back uncomfortably and handed her a ten-dollar bill. She ripped it out of my hand and after a few moments gave me my change back. I walked towards the furthest table away from her. I wanted to avoid her at all costs. The bar was filled with drunk fat white trash men in their fifties who liked to talk about cars, sex, and women. Everything felt a little bit too familiar.

I sat down at a small circular table all the way in the back of the bar. This was the furthest away I could get from that rude elephant woman bartender, and from those loud drunk men. I leaned back on my chair and gave my first official legal Budweiser a sip. Budweiser was what Jimmy used to drink. I missed Jimmy. And I have been missing him every day since he jumped off the cliff on Christmas Eve. I missed Jimmy's body wrapped around my body. I missed Jimmy's galaxy blue eyes. I missed the feeling of Jimmy inside of me. Since his suicide, I have always wondered why I have never been able to stop loving him. Why I have never been able to forget him. Why I have never been able to truly move on. If he treated me like a disposable piece of trash, then why I did get so obsessed? And why am I still obsessed to this very day? Because there isn't a morning where I don't wake up to the thought of Jimmy. Or a night where I don't imagine myself laying on Jimmy's chest whilst I rest my head on my pillow. Ever since he killed himself, I have been unable to wash off the fingerprints and marks he left on my body. He never got the opportunity to cleanse or eradicate the crimes he committed on me.

I started working at the 'Texan Drive In' right after Jimmy's death. I used to work here every weekend in the last semester of my senior year. And stayed here for two years before leaving for Arizona State University. After finishing high school, I was unable to go to college straight away because Mother and Father were having trouble with mortgages and money debts and didn't have enough money to send me to college. After two years, my parents were able to pay off their debts and I was able to fix the problems I had with my Federal Student Aid. I was then able to move to Phoenix for college.

From the age of eighteen to the age of twenty I stayed in Corpus Christi and spent most of my nights working at 'The Texan Drive In'. It was rough. And I was very unhappy. I can still remember the smell of piss and urine when I used to clean the male bathrooms after the end of my shift. Nowadays, the smell of public bathroom urine reminds me of how I used to cry to the thought of Jimmy when I used to mop the floors of the toilets. The stench of beer and malt that consumed the whole bar reminded me of the many times I used to spill Coors Light and Blue Moon into my shoes and pants after getting distracted to the sentiment of Jimmy fucking my asshole. The scent of the pine-fragranced floor detergent I used to mop the ale-pissed corners of the bar brought me back to the pain I felt whenever I would hear Jimmy's grunting and voice inside my head when I used to close the bar by myself. I still remember walking back home crying through the streets near Baldwin Avenue at 4AM after my tiring and draining shift at work, and how I used to walk past random motels and hotels wishing I could resuscitate Jimmy from the dead, and wishing he would take me to Room 301 in 'La Santa Espina' motel again. I remember screaming in the middle of those streets under tall streetlamps: *"COME BAAAAACCCCKKKK!"* But Jimmy never magically appeared. I would then end up in the middle of the sidewalk crying all scrunched up on the floor every single time.

On my third shift at 'The Texan Drive In', my ugly fat manager derogatively called me a 'dirty Mexican'. His name was Andrew. He was white, bald and racist. He liked to call me 'a dirty Mexican' whenever I would make a mistake, spill a drink or mix up an order. It was extremely depreciatory and belittling. But no one ever defended me. All of the other staff members were accomplices to his racist and discriminatory attacks. They were all small-dick white supremacist fuckers.

As I went through my Budweiser, I observed the staff members who worked behind the bar and felt relieved that I was no longer working here. I felt alleviated to know that those racist remarks and long working hours no longer consumed my life. It felt good to come here after a long while to make peace with this place and realise how much I have grown as a person since I left more than a year ago. I no longer was that weak and frail little Mexican eighteen-year-old boy.

The tacky fat wench with smudged eyeliner that had served me on the bar earlier reminded me of the other white supremacist cunt I used to work with. Beth. A narcissistic, closeted alcoholic. When I used to work with her, I tried to avoid her at all costs because her breath would stink like fermented raw fish from all the red wine bottles she would drink throughout the shift. She was scary to look at. She was balding and had hair growing in her lower chin, probably a symptom of Polycystic

Ovary Syndrome. I had never met such a violent and masculine woman as her. She probably had more testosterone in her system than I ever did. She liked to make me cry because I was young, and she was insecure.

Beth once screamed at me in the wine cellar downstairs after fucking up an order. She used to call me *'good-for-nothing'* and *'worthless'*. And when someone keeps referring to you with those words repeatedly, it slowly starts getting into your head and you start believing it. I still remember how she then sent me upstairs after her aggressive rant to keep pouring drinks, and how I was unable to conceal my tremor and turbulence in front of bawdy white manly customers. Tears kept streaming down my face uncontrollably. Beth then took me aside right away after she had realised that customers were aware that I was crying right in front of them. She snatched my arms, took me outside through the backdoor, and coldly briefed me.

"You are a big boy now. No more tears." I could see the anger in her eyes. The veins around her irises popping off.

"You are an adult now. Welcome to the real world. Big boys don't cry," she cruelly remarked.

But she didn't have to welcome me to the real world. I already knew what it was. I already knew what cruelty and ruthlessness was. I had already experienced rejection and emotional abandonment from my mother. I had already experienced what it was like to see the dismembered corpse of someone you never got to say *'I love you'* to in person before they left. She didn't have to give me a patronizing lecture of what it was to be an adult. I knew everything about it. I knew how this world worked. I knew that this world was brutal and unmerciful ever since I was young, and Mother locked me in the cupboard of the basement for twelve hours straight. I knew that neither God nor Jesus gave a fuck about me or anyone on this planet. They were just a created illusion to help stupid people like my mother find a meaning to their own boring and mundane life.

"No one cares if you are crying or not. Get a grip and keep

working. Customers don't pay to watch stupid boys like you cry," she heartlessly stated.

I wiped the tears off my cheeks, and blew my nose with my fingers, smudging my snot on the side of my pants.

"Suck it up! I'm not here to babysit eighteen-year-olds!"

I nodded and looked down. She briskly opened the backdoor and went inside. I breathed in and out and got ready to get back to work. This was the real world. This was America. There was no work ethic. No one cared about you. Not even one soul. I wondered why I still hadn't developed thick skin after everything I had endured in the past. *Was I just sensitive?', 'Was I just emotionally overburnt?', 'Did my tolerance for rejection finally come to an end?', 'Why did older people keep picking on me?', 'Why were all the tyrannical authorities in my life always trying to make me feel undeserving and unworthy?'*

I have always been accustomed to older men disrespecting me. All my life, that is all I have ever known. I have been forced to suck dicks I've never wanted to suck. I have been obligated to open my ass cheeks against my desire not to. I have been touched and groped without my consent. My body has never belonged to me, it has always belonged to them. Whenever an older man would touch me without my consent, it would ruthlessly bring me back to the moment when Father Orlando raped me. The moment I never ever want to go back to. Because the memory of him makes me freeze to death every time someone or something reminds me of him.

I once had a really bad panic attack during one of my shifts. I can still recall the 57-year-old man that came up to me and told me that my Wrangler bootcut jeans looked *'nice and tight'* around my ass. Throughout my shift, he kept staring at my ass whilst he sipped his bitter Guinness, and I wiped and cleared tables. It made me feel extremely uncomfortable. But most significantly, it made me feel like Father Orlando was spying on me with his evil reptile eyes. So, I took my manager Andrew to the backdoor immediately to address this matter. I could hardly breathe and babbled nonsensical words. I was trying to explain to him why this man had made me feel uneasy and uncomfortable, and why he had made me feel anxious. But he didn't understand, nor did he want to. He was racist. He hated Mexicans. And the least he wanted to do was to deal with my *'delirious'* problems.

"He's a regular. He's drunk. Leave him alone and suck it up," he brutally retaliated.

No one cared. No one knew why this certain man was making me feel this way. And no one took the time to understand either. Because no one knew that I had been brutally raped at the age of fifteen. No one knew that my rapist's shadow followed me everywhere I went. This 57-year-old man looked like Father Orlando. He was bald. He was fat. And he was ugly. But maybe I was reading into it too much. Maybe I was going crazy and delusional. Maybe he didn't mean it. Maybe he was just joking. Maybe he was just in fact drunk. *'Why did I always tend to make everything about myself?', 'Was I just being selfish and self-absorbed?', 'Were the symptoms of my traumas narcissistically manifesting themselves into the present?'*

Hunter, the 57-year-old man magically started to appear in all my shifts. I started to feel extremely unsafe and vulnerable. *'Was this just a coincidence or did he have hidden intentions?'* I didn't know why this man was interested in me, and why he kept staring at me repeatedly every time he came to the bar.

That night, the 25th of April 1995 was when things started to take an unexpected turn. After kicking out all our bawdy and obscene customers at 3:00AM, I had to mop the floors, wipe the tables, clean the bathrooms and clean the bar with Beth. Our shift officially finished at 4:00AM. After getting my vintage light-brown caramel leather jacket and my navy-blue Jansport backpack from the staffroom, I walked out of the backdoor like any other day. Beth had already left. But to my surprise, Hunter, the 57-year-old-man, was waiting there with a cigarette in his mouth. My heart started to palpitate really fast. I didn't know what to do or what to say. I wanted to walk past right him, but I also didn't want to be rude. But this was the same man that had said that my Wrangler bootcut jeans looked good around my ass. *'Why the fuck was I going to say hi to him?', 'Why the fuck was he waiting on the backdoor?'* He certainly wasn't waiting for anybody else, but me.

"Hey, buddy," he charmingly said, exhaling tobacco smoke from his mouth.

'Fuck.', 'He's talking to me now.' My hands started to tremble. *'Run! Tony! Run!'* There were no customers left in the parking lot. There was no one there. We were the only people left. It was just him and I stuck and trapped in the back of the building. I was in big trouble. I was stranded. Like a predator, he was ready to feast on his prey.

"Hi," I forcefully smiled, trying to avoid looking at him.

"Where you after?" he vulgarly rested his left hand above his western buckle belt and then clutched his protruding bulge.

"I'm going home…"

"You driving there? —"

"No-I'm walking," I nervously interrupted.

"Can I drive you there?"

"No… I'm fine-thanks," I fearfully answered, accepting the fact that something really dark was about to happen.

It was pitch-black and there was only one streetlamp on the other side of the parking lot illuminating this macabre and gruesome setting.

"You are really handsome, you know…" He tossed his cigarette onto the concrete floor and stepped on it with his right foot. He started to caress his bulge more eminently. I could tell he was drunk, and his breath smelled like utter junk. My thoughts were racing, and my vision was starting to blur. There was no way to escape this situation.

"Thank you," I looked down at the ground.

"Can I ask you something weird?"

I stayed silent.

"Would you ever suck my dick?" he casually asked with his disgusting whiskey breath.

I breathed in and out. *'This can't be happening to me again.'*

"No," I firmly countered. I started to walk but then he quickly hijacked my arm, stopping me from going anywhere.

"How much do you want?"

"Nothing. I just want to go home." My fight-or-flight response started to activate.

"I have cash with me," he reached towards his pocket and took out a fat stash of money. Green greedy capitalist American dollars.

I looked down at the pile of cash dangling on his hand. I felt triggered. But tempted. "I'm going home."

"Wait—" He gripped my wrist.

"What?"

He started to flicker through the bills. And although I was feeling extremely anxious and uneasy, the way he shuffled the cash between his hands hypnotized me. Suddenly, I had forgotten about everything. I became dumb and hollow-headed. My eyes were bewitched by the prize. My eyes glistened. I had never felt anything like this before. But I had to be smart and rational. And although the offer was alluring, I had to decline it and run home. "Please. I just want to go home," I rapidly answered. I felt uncomfortable and endangered.

"200. Come on."

"No. Nothing. I don't want anything!" I angrily replied.

"300!"

"No!"

"350!"

"No!" I resisted. But then everything changed in the blink of an eye. There was only one thing that would be able to change my mind. This man was drunk, and I figured that if he wanted to take advantage of me, I was also going to take advantage of him. "Give me everything you have."

"No come on, that's 700!" he childishly threw his arms into the air.

"700 or NOTHING!" I looked at his eyes with utter anger and disgust on my face because he was the one that put us into this situation.

He looked down at his stash of dough and counted each banknote carefully. He breathed in deeply and audibly sighed. He handed me the stash. "Deal."

I counted the cash meticulously, making sure that each bill counted to 700 dollars. It did in fact all add up to 700. "Okay," I loudly exhaled and crammed the cash inside my pocket. I was in disbelief that I was actually doing this.

"Let's go to my car," he placed his hand behind my lower back and walked me towards his car.

This was the first time I was going to prostitute myself. This was the first time I was going to sell my body like that. This was the first time I was going to sell my soul to the Devil.

We were both scrunched up in the backseat of his car. His car smelled like piss and rancid tobacco. The floors were dirty, and the nylon cloth seats were cum-stained. He rapidly took his belt off and pulled his jeans down. His foul and repulsive erection protruded through his red-striped boxers. He forcefully pulled my head down.

"Take my boxers off," he violently caterwauled.

I had already been broken inside. I didn't want to break apart even more. My broken china legs and arms hadn't been glued together just yet. History was repeating itself. This was going to haunt me for the rest of my life. I breathed in and out and pulled his boxers off. His penis swung up into my face.

"Suck that big fat cock!" he grunted like a boorish ogre.

I looked down on it. It was scary and frightening. It smelled like a rotten swamp. His untrimmed pubic hair was sprinkled with dead skin cells. I hesitated; I wasn't ready to do this.

"Come on, suck it," he grabbed my head and aggressively pulled it towards his pelvic area.

His penis was inside my mouth. It was long and thick, and it tasted like stinking fish. He pulled my head down back and forth in a volatile manner. He was brutishly yanking my hair, which made the back of my neck hurt. He pounded his penis inside my mouth, and I started to choke. It was hard to breathe, and every time it went all the way to the back of my mouth to my tonsils, I gagged. I wanted to puke. His penis kept going in back and forth. And the best thing I could do was to try to close my eyes and block it from my mind. I didn't know what I was doing. I was dissociating.

"No teeth, you fucker," he brutally slapped my face, leaving a red mark on my cheeks.

I kept sucking it and he kept grunting. His hairy belly kept thrusting against my nose and eyes. He grabbed me by the neck and started to press on it ferociously. He started to growl, almost as if he was about to ejaculate.

"Not yet!" he smacked my face once again.

I was being brutally abused and beaten up. This wasn't new. I had already experienced this exact same thing in the past. This was historic recurrence. And I really wanted this to end. But he kept pushing his throbbing penis inside my mouth relentlessly. I was starting to get tired. My hands were getting swamped with tears, snot and saliva.

69

"Turn around!" he remorselessly exclaimed.

"What?"

"I said turn around. I'm going to fuck you!"

I looked up at him with fright and terror. I didn't sign up for this. I started to hyperventilate. I thought I was just going to suck his dick and that was going to be it. This can't be happening again. I could feel the venom inside my veins reaching towards my brain. I started to cry and sob. It all felt very intense. My chest started to tighten, and my arms started to inhumanly shake. Tears started to flood the interior of the car. I didn't want this. I didn't want this again. He had already paid me. I couldn't say no. But we had only agreed that I was going suck his dick. He never said anything about fucking.

My vision started to obfuscate. Everything started to move in slow motion. I no longer was inside my body. My soul had already dissipated. I was just a dead piece of meat about to get raped. I started to cry even harder. This ruthlessly reminded me of Father Orlando. *'Why was this happening to me again?', 'Why did God like to put me in these situations?'*

He ripped my Wrangler bootcuts off.

"HEEEEEEEEELPPPPPPP!" I cried out. But no one could hear me.

He grabbed me from the back of my head and chucked me towards the window. He savagely pushed my face and cheeks against the glass. My neck was twisted. Air could hardly travel through my trachea.

"Shut up you little bitch! I paid you!" He pulled my hair even harder. "You scream again, and I'm going to fucking kill you!" He spanked my ass cheeks barbarically.

This is what happens when you make a pact with the Devil. The Devil always finds a way to defraud you. This was a hoax sent directly from hell. But I just wanted to get it over with as soon as possible. The impact this was going to have on me on the future was going to be unbearable. This was when I pitilessly learnt that money doesn't in fact buy happiness, because not even a million dollars will help you forget how brutally you got raped.

Tears fell onto the nylon-clothed car seat. I felt a huge void in my chest and felt like I was going to faint. I closed my eyes and tried to think about something else. But I was unable to. He tore my boxers off and cold-heartedly put his long-nailed finger up my anus.

"You ready to take it?" He stroked his penis back and forth whilst he fingered my ass hole.

I remained silent. I couldn't answer. I was frozen and petrified. At this point I was just a corpse, and he was a necrophiliac.

"I'm going to fuck you up!" He whacked my ass cheeks once again. This time I could feel a purple bruise growing on my left ass cheek from how hard he hit me.

He slid his penis right inside of me without warning me before. I squealed out of pain. It hurt. It was dry, and there was no lubricant to ease the pain. The skin of his penis rubbed the inside of my rectum, which caused strife and friction. He was harming me. He kept drilling me harder and harder, making sure his penis went deeply inside of me. I was vociferously sobbing. Snot ran all the way down into my mouth. He grabbed me by the neck and primitively bit it.

"OUCH!" I screamed. I hit his face with the palm of my hand.

He bit me harder and started to choke me. His hands and fingers gripped my throat and windpipe tightly. I could feel the violence and anger in his volatile actions. He spat on my back.

"You like that?"

I was unable to breathe. I could start to feel my heartbeat getting slower and slower. I didn't want to die, but at the same time I did. He kept pounding me as he strangled me. You could hear it in his voice, he was enjoying every little bit of it. I started to lose my hearing and started to see blinking dots in the air. I was finally going to die.

He thankfully let go of his hands on my neck. He probably felt that I was starting to daze off and I was going purple. He twisted my neck and kissed me. He put his tongue down my throat. He hostilely kept piercing my ass with his penis from the back. He started to groan louder and louder. Sweat from his forehead dropped onto my back. I could tell that he was about to cum. He kept fucking me harder and harder. He grabbed me from the back of my head and put his forehead on my collarbone, he was about to reach climax.

He ejaculated inside of me. He loudly exhaled and slipped his slimy penis off my rectum. It hurt. It really hurt. I could feel my anal tissues bleeding. I had just gotten violently raped. I gasped for breath, but I could hardly breathe. He recomposed himself and moved away from me. He grabbed his red striped boxers and wiped the semen from his penis. I couldn't believe it. *Why was I still alive?' 'What was I going to do?'* I was just going to have to keep silent and move on with my life like nothing had ever happened. The same way I lived my life after Father Orlando raped me. *'Where were God and Jesus to save me from these barbarous and violent situations?', 'Why did they let this happen?', 'Was it because I was a homosexual and this is what I deserved?', 'Did I deserve to be tortured and raped until the day of my death?', 'Was this the hell I had to go through to go to heaven?'*

"Fuck me, you were so tight," he chuckled.

I stayed silent. My long hair was on my face. I wanted to leave right away. So, I grabbed my white linen boxers and my Wranglers. I hurriedly put them on, snatched my leather jacket and backpack from the floor, and opened the car door.

"Do you want a drive home?" he politely asked, like if he hadn't just raped me moments before.

I got out of the car and harshly slammed the door. I started to walk back home. I reached towards my pocket and took out the 700-dollar stash. I clenched it and put it back on my pocket. After a few moments, I heard his car pull up next to me.

He rolled the car window down.

"See yaw, motherfuckeeeeeeeeer!!!" he childishly bawled, putting his tongue out. His car speedily left zooming through the streets.

It was about 6AM and I could start to hear the morning birds. I could hardly walk or breathe. Every little part of my body hurt. I was destroyed. Someone in Corpus Christi had wrecked and destroyed me once again. I was going to have to swallow an experience like this again and never be able to talk about it to anyone. I was going to have to go back home, and Mother was going to still treat me the same. She was still going to scorn me and talk to me like her servant. She was still going to talk to me in her rude and narcissistic manners. I had absolutely no one to go cry to. Not even God or Jesus. I didn't have Jimmy's chest to rest my face and cry on either. I was alone. Truly. Fucking. Alone. I dropped my knees onto the floor and surrendered. I shrieked and screamed. I cried and wept. I scratched my arms with my feisty nails. I was panting and wheezing. I looked up at the sky. The first appearance of light shone across the grey melancholic clouds. It was dawn. I kept crying. The salt of my tears eroded the skin of my cheeks. I clenched my hands together at the height of my chest and tried to speak to Jesus.

"I'm sorry Jesus. I *really* am sorry," I murmured, aware of the fact that I was speaking to nobody but the air.

"I didn't choose to be like this. I promise," I grabbed myself from the neck. Almost as if I was trying to strangle myself.

"Why do these things keep happening to me, Jesus?"

No answer.

There was never going to be an answer to that.

I stopped working at the 'Texan Drive In' after that wicked and immoral night. I never showed up to any of my shifts ever again. I stopped answering any of my managers' calls and decided that I would never go to that place ever again in my life. I decided I was going to suppress that experience like all the others. When I got to my house that morning, I decided that I was never going to allow myself to process it and I was never going to speak about it to anyone. I decided I was going to incarcerate all these traumatic memories and experiences inside an iron-safe box and throw them all the way into the deep ocean. And ever since I tossed it into the sea, I have been scared that it could float up to the surface again at any given point in time in the present.

But this was the summer where that iron-safe box had magically floated up again from the dark depths of the ocean into the surface. This 21st birthday was when I finally decided that I wanted to open that iron-safe box again and shrewdly face my past.

I thought I was never going to be able to come back to the 'Texan Drive In' ever again in my life after I got raped here. But having my first official legal Budweiser in this place as a celebration for my 21st birthday had to be one of the most challenging and audacious things I had ever done in my life. Life is extremely unexpected, and you must learn to take it as it comes with no expectations. This place was still the same. Nothing had changed. Except the staff members. The same bawdy and loud white fifty-year old men customers were still there. The regulars were still there. The smell of piss and stringent ale was still existent. The neon light signs behind the bar still flickered and trembled the same way they did when I used to work here. The floors were still sticky. And the tables were still rugged and viscid. The bar still had the same selection of beers. And the chefs still spat on customers' burgers before they got served. Everything was still the same. I was the only one that had changed.

I gently slammed the glass on the table after I finished my Budweiser and reached for my car keys in the front pocket of my jeans. I stood up and walked towards the front door. I said goodbye to the fat ugly tacky wench that rudely served me and walked out. I walked through the parking lot where I was once brutishly raped. The sun was starting to set. The skies were pink-blushed orange. A classic Texan summer sunset. I opened the door of my car and sat on the driver's seat. This was the summer where I was going to have to face everything I had been repressing all my life. I looked up at the cotton candy clouds through the windshield and wondered what it would be like to fall in love again. I wondered what it would be like to find someone that would understand me and my past. I contemplated on what it would feel like to be loved. Maybe this was the summer I was going to find someone. Maybe this was the summer I was going to find someone that was going to help me face my past. I turned the engine on and clutched the stirring wheel nervously. *'Where was I going to go next?'*

V

Salvador Perez Public Swimming Pool

John 4:18

"There is no fear in love, but perfect love casts out fear.
For fear has to do with punishment,
and whoever fears has not been perfected in love."

Waking up in the middle of the night to go to the bathroom, I wish I had a manly chest to lie my head on after pissing. A warm masculine body to keep me warm. It is the 3rd of August 1996, and it is 4AM. The window of my room is wide open, trying to let the gust of wind freshen my putridly humid room. It is impossible to fall asleep in this heat. August is one of the hottest months in Texas. The air conditioner inside my room doesn't work and it has almost been three summers since Mother decided not to pay for someone to come and fix it. Although I have a ceiling fan above my bed, it only works to make annoying loud zooming noises. It doesn't eradicate any type of heat.

I like to sleep naked. I like to let my penis and testicles hang freely with no restriction. I don't sleep with any covers on, and although I want to hug a pillow whilst I sleep to feel like I'm lying on a man's chest, it is too warm to do so.

When the heat wakes me up in the middle of the night, I like to look at how the ceiling fan spins around in circles. I like to get stuck in that trance and wonder what it would be like to have someone next to me. Ever since I was a twelve, I have always romanticized what it would be like to have a summer fling. What it would be like to fall in love in the summer and then break up before going back to college. I've always wanted to go through that torture and pain. The type of heartbreak and grief only a summer love could give you. I wanted to have sex in public pool toilets. I wanted to make out with someone under the moonlight and stars on the coarse and dry grasslands across the 181. I wanted to be held. I wanted to be loved. I hadn't been touched for more than three months, and I wanted to be touched. I wanted someone to help me make sense of my life. I wanted someone to help me carry all the pain and trauma I had been carrying on my shoulders all by myself my entire life. I hate all that nonsensical bullshit that everyone says, "You can't love other people until you love yourself," or the "Learn to love yourself first, instead of loving the idea of other people loving you." No. Fuck that. Did I love myself? Maybe not. Did I want to be loved? Yes. Did I want to process all my past traumas and troubles by my own? No. Did I want someone help me carry my emotional baggage? Yes.

I met Axel at the Salvador Perez Public Swimming Pool on the afternoon of the 3rd of August. Apart from going to watch horror films in the movie theatre by myself, writing in my room all day and eating on the trunk of my car, I also enjoyed going for a little swim in the afternoons to the public pool near my house. In the gay world of the nineties, public pools were a good spot to find someone to cruise with. And although I went to the pool to swim, I was never against the idea of potentially hooking up with someone from there. If the opportunity arose, then I'd take it. But my only rule was that I wouldn't initiate anything. I would only wait for someone to talk to me and make a move. Because this was the summer I was going to desperately stop seeking male sexual validation or attention from anyone. I was going to take things as they came. I wasn't going to force anything to happen.

The Salvador Perez Public Swimming Pool was a beautifully looking pool. It was a massive rectangular pool with an average depth, surrounded with plastic white sun beds and navy-blue nylon umbrellas. It was next to the 544 freeway. And although cars and trucks zoomed right past it, the cacti and palm trees outside the establishment made it look like an American Saharan Paradise. The smell of Banana Boat sunscreen and Hawaiian Tropic tanning oil consumed this whole infernal atmosphere.

I rested my back on an inclined sun bed. I was wearing my baby-blue, butt-short swimming trunks and my vintage tortoiseshell Ray-ban wayfarers. My skin was golden-scorched and the brown hairs on my legs and arms had turned flamed blonde. I was writing in my notebook and smoking a gold-infused Lucky Strike cigarette. I was writing a poem that came to my mind when I was swimming in the pool. I was taking in the rays of sunlight and minding my own business. The sky was clear neon blue and the place itself was rather empty. It was about 5PM, and the only other two people in the establishment were an old lady sunbathing, and the lifeguard who was seating on his lifeguard tower right in front of me across the pool. I always thought that lifeguards were only hot, beautiful and sexy on the silver screen, I never thought any of the lifeguards in real life could be as gorgeous and attractive as the ones in the movies. But Axel was.

Axel, the lifeguard right in front of me, was wearing a tight crimson-red tee with a white cross on the middle of his bulky chest. His short penny-pinched red swimming trunks showed off his big muscular thighs and protruding bulge. He had beautiful greasy long hazel hair that dropped all the way to his shoulders. His arms were beefy and corpulent. His face was chiselled, and his sharp chin and jawline were adorned with a spikey prickly stubble. A stubble I couldn't wait to get my ass cheeks on. His brown eyebrows, almost black, were thick and bushy like mine. His big roman nose with a bump in its bridge, gave him character and made him look even more butch and masculine than he was. His eyes were emerald green and sparkled like a sharp diamond hidden at the bottom of a gold mine. Although his lips were thin and dry, his teeth were straight and paper white. If Jimmy had been birthed by the ancient Greeks and the Blonde Goddess, Axel had been conceived by the Romans and carved like a heroic marble sculpture holding a decapitated lion's head. But instead of holding a lion's head, he was holding mine.

Axel was sucking on a Firecracker Ice Pop. He was viciously lost in his thoughts. I had to put my notebook over my crotch as the way his mouth and lips suckled and munched on the popsicle made me get an erection. I wanted to suck his penis in the same fervent and passionate way he was sucking on his ice lolly. I couldn't stop staring at him. Something about his physique and face captured me. I was drowning on a pool of lust and infatuation, and I wanted him to come and save me. I started sweating, and not because of the extreme Texan heat, but because I was nervous to be around him. After a few moments, I started to feel desolate and sad. And that always happened when I lusted after a man in public. I would firstly get mesmerised and infatuated, and then I would have to quickly remind myself that there was no way in this world that that man would ever get to kiss me and fuck me. He was so painfully hot, and it made me exceptionally angry. A beautiful, gorgeous, handsome man always disoriented my sense of confidence. I was struggling to distinguish whether I was falling in love with him or if I wanted to be him. If anything, Axel had just ruined my summer. I was ready to go home and cry under my covers to the thought of how single and lonely I was. Axel was the first person ever since Jimmy, that with one look could make me feel butterflies in my stomach and could make me get an erection underneath my pants.

The old lady that was sunbathing six sun beds away from mine started to pack her stuff away. She put her damp towel and book inside her Mexican palm straw bag. She put a silk chiffon slip in dress over her black opaque swimsuit. And slipped her stubby feet on her sandals. She promptly left. Axel and I were the only people left in the place. It was about 6PM and the pool was magically empty. The pool was going to close in an hour. And I was going to stay in my sun bed until he'd come and talk to me. I had a feeling that he had been observing me whilst I was swimming in the pool, and then later journaling in my sun bed.

But maybe I was just being delusional, as I had always tended to be.

I first noticed him because I felt like someone was looking at me. And it certainly wasn't the old lady as she was too bothered reading her own book. It was him while he sucked his ice lolly. When I got out of the pool to reach for my towel on the sun bed, I looked back on him, and I could tell he was staring at my ass. Yes. My short baby-blue swimming trunks that made my ass look bigger and perkier than it actually was. It was clear that if I was infatuated with his arms, thighs, and bulge, he was bewitched by my peachy ass and feminine chivalrous face.

I kept writing on my notebook. And to be honest, at this point I was just jotting random shit on paper. I was trying to look occupied and natural. He was probably wondering why I hadn't left yet as I had been there for more than five hours. The sun was still shining bright. But fortunately, no human soul had showed up again. It was still only the two of us.

I looked up at him. He was staring at me. With a dead-pan face, he was looking directly at me. *'Fuck. Is he is actually looking at me?', 'Maybe this can go somewhere.', 'Okay Tony, you got this.'* I left my chest shirtless and like a male peacock with regal colourful feathers, I let the tanning oil on my muscles do the job. I opened my legs wide open and showed him my bulge. I kept writing on my notebook and although cringe, I tried to look mysterious. I swiftly took a gold-infused Lucky strike from my cigarette pack and placed it on my lips. Nervous and startled, I tried to look for my lighter in my bag. I tucked my hair behind my ears and looked up again towards the lifeguard tower. He no longer was there. *'Where was he?'* He was walking towards me. My heart started to thump faster and faster. I recomposed myself and tried to act as naturally as possible. I clumsily put the cigarette back on the packet. And I tried to act like I hadn't been thinking of him for the past five hours. I tried to act like I hadn't already gone to the public bathroom and masturbated to the thought of him fucking me.

"Hey man," he said in a masculine tone of voice.

"Hi," I looked up from my notebook and casually smiled.

"Just letting you know that we close the pool at 7PM."

"Yeah, I know," my voice gingerly cracked.

"Cool. Just wanted to check, because you are the last one here, and I could honestly close the pool right now and go home. It's been really quiet, and I have been here since the morning."

"Oh, sorry. Do you want me to leave?"

"Do whatever you want," he blatantly chuckled.

"I mean. If you want to close the pool, I can just grab my stuff and go." I could hardly feel my heart and I could feel my mouth drying up. I didn't know where this was going, but I didn't have a great feeling about it.

"What's your name?" he said with a softer quality of voice.

"Antonio. Well, I go by Tony."

"Axel," he gently offered me his hand, "nice to meet you."

I shook it shyly.

"I've never seen you before. Do you live close by?"

"Yes. I live two blocks away. In Santa Marta Close—"

"No wayyyy! I live on the road next to yours. Brownville road." A smile started to grow on his face.

"Oh, nice," I nervously giggled. I didn't know what else to say.

"What are you writing?"

"Oh, nothing. I usually just write stupid poems or little stories here and there... Nothing special."

"Really? Stupid? What stupid things have you been writing all day then?" He got closer to me. "I've been observing you," he subtly smirked.

81

"I mean it's been a boring day. I like to sunbathe, I guess." I wasn't making any sense.

"I know why you've spent your whole day here."

"Uh......" This conversation was starting to go somewhere.

"Apart from staring at your notebook, I've been the other person you've been staring at... Tell me, do I have something on my face?"

'Fuck.', 'He knew that I was looking at him all along.' "No-no-um-ha, ha, I mean there weren't much other people to look at."

"Take your sunglasses off. Let me see those eyes," he firmly demanded.

I took my vintage tortoiseshell wayfarers off and looked directly into his piercing green eyes. I could feel the boner growing underneath my baby-blue swimming trunks. The sexual tension was growing. And the only thing that was holding us apart from screwing each other was the fact that we were in an exterior public area.

"You have beautiful eyes," he said, subtly biting his lip.

"Thank you," I timorously laughed.

"How old are you?"

"I'm 21... And you?"

"I'm 24."

"Oh—"

"What?"

"Nothing, nothing," I couldn't control my laughter.

"I'm only 3 years older than you. What are you saying??!"

"I didn't say anything. Ha-ha," I tried to avoid eye contact.

"Are you Mexican?"

"Umm... my grandparents were... But I was born here."

"Mexican people are one of the most beautiful people on earth."

"You think?

"Yeah, just look at your eyebrows and the colour of your skin."

"Thank you." My cheeks started to blush. "You are really kind."

"You are gay, right?" he embarrassingly asked.

"Um, well..." I was puzzled. No one had ever asked me that before. "I guess so... but I haven't really told anyone. My parents, you know, they would be funny about it and would probably kick me out of the house if they knew." We both laughed. "Are you?"

"Ummm... Good question... I don't know... I just broke up with my girlfriend a few weeks ago. I've always thought guys were hot and I have always kind of suppressed it... When I saw you looking at me, it made me think, you know what, maybe I *should* experiment."

"Well, yeah, I guess there is a first for everything." We both laughed even louder. The tension between us was getting more and more intense. He walked closer to me. His penis was at the height of my face. Something was clearly about to happen.

"I think I know what you want..." He scratched the back of his head and nervously checked behind him if there was anyone around.

"What?" I looked up at him, but I could only see his masculine voluptuous peachy ass.

He turned around and looked directly into my eyes. "My dick," he said, as he subtly started to caress the outline of his penis with his thick virile fingers. I had never felt that excruciating feeling on my chest ever before. The way he looked directly at me whilst he gently gripped his balls violated every piece of my inner privacy and intimacy.

83

My mouth rapidly moved back and forth around his erected pulsating penis. We were both locked inside the accessible bathroom for disabled people in the locker rooms of the pool. He tightly grasped the back of my neck with his Muhammad Ali boxing hands and eagerly pushed his cock in and out of my mouth. I was worshipping what I had been waiting to worship since I first caught eye contact with him. I was on my knees, and he was on his feet. I jerked his dick off with my left hand whilst I tickled the tip of his penis with my tongue. He grunted and groaned like a ferocious man. He liked what I was doing to him. I was way better than his ex-girlfriend. I rolled my eyes backwards as he penetrated his dick deeply into my mouth. He had a thick, veiny, cock and colossal hanging testicles that swinged back and forth against my chin as he furiously mouth fucked me. I stroked my own penis as I sucked him. This no longer existed in the constraints of my own imagination. This was real. I was masturbating to the real, materialized action of him.

I liked the taste of his penis and the smell of his sweat. He pounded my face harder and harder with every go. The skin on his forehead started to scrunch up as he started to audibly moan.

"You are so good," he grabbed me by the head.

I looked up at him with dainty honeysuckle eyes.

"You are going to make me cum," he moaned again.

So, I grabbed his dick and sucked it even harder. Making sure it went deep, deep, inside the inner corners my mouth.

He forcefully scratched my shoulders with his nails and boisterously growled.

"Cum for me," I said, piercing him with a submissive and subordinate look in my eyes.

"Can I cum in your face?"

"Yeah," I grabbed both of his testicles with my left hand and subtly shook them side by side.

"Uh-uh-uh. Aughhhhh!" he orgasmed. He splattered all of his

fervent warm semen on my face. I liked the sensation of a warm slippery fluid dripping across my nose and cheeks. I wiped the cum out of my face with my hands and licked it off my fingers.

"Mmmmmm…" he mumbled.

He leaned down and kissed me. We shared a long kiss. He put his tongue inside my mouth. And I put mine on his. I stood up after the kiss and hugged him. I pressed my sweaty chest against his.

"That was good," he theatrically sighed.

"Yeah," I laughed and wiped the saliva out of my lips with the interior side of my wrist.

Both of our naked bodies were intrinsically latched to each other.

"What are you doing tonight?" he asked, with both of his ungodly sinful hands on my naked devilish lower back.

I stood silent for a second. I couldn't believe what he had just asked me. I thought sucking him off was going to be the end of our story. But I was wrong. "Nothing."

He smiled. "Do you want to go to Johnny B's Outlaw Saloon tonight?"

"Sure," I quickly replied, not really knowing what he meant by it. *'Is he asking me out on a date?'* My catholic-constrained mind loudly echoed.

"There is a mechanical bull…" he said, trying to persuade me to go, as he wiped the last drop of his bittersweet semen from my left earlobe with his thumb and index finger, smearing into my lips.

I laughed and licked it off with my tongue.

VI

The Mechanical Bull

2 Corinthians 6:14

"Do not be yoked together with unbelievers.
For what do righteousness and wickedness
have in common?
Or what fellowship can light have with darkness?"

It was about 9PM and I was waiting for him outside 'Johnny B's Outlaw Saloon'. Before coming here, I went back home for a quick and cold shower after that hot-sweaty-sexy session I had with Axel in the accessible bathroom of the pool. I was wearing a black Marlboro leather jacket I stole from Quique's closet, followed by my classic Wrangler faded blue bootcut jeans that lifted and compressed my ass into a beautiful circular shape. I also had a tight white tee on that showed off my well-built pectorals and biceps. And a pair of caramel, brown-leathered high top Converse Chucks. My hair was left greasy and unwashed, and I styled it like Johnny Ramone from The Ramones.

I wasn't nervous anymore as I had already had his cock inside my mouth. I was thrilled and excited to know that apart from already having the opportunity to kiss him and giving him a blow job, he was taking me out on a proper formal date. It was going to be my first official legal date since I turned twenty-one. No one had ever taken me out to a bar before, let alone the 'Johnny B's Outlaw Saloon'.

Axel got out of his cherry-red Volkswagen Jetta and roughly slammed the door shut. He was wearing a denim-on-denim set. He was wearing a pair of bootcut jeans. We were twinning. His

86

chest and bodice were sexily displayed with a black tight turtleneck that went underneath a baggy denim jacket adorned with an array of colourful pins. His alluring silky long hair had been blow-dried. He had a pair of black leather cowboy boots which had a metal steel ending on each boot. It made him look taller and overall edgier. He was trying to look good. He was trying to look good for *me*. And that made me happy. I smiled at him and waved hello as he approached me.

"Well, hello, Mister," he gently padded me on the back, trying to hide the fact that he was attracted to me.

"Hello." We caught eye contact. "You smell good…"

"What can I say?" He flicked his hair flamboyantly. "You've been waiting here for long?" He put the car keys that dangled on his fingers inside the front pocket of his jeans.

"Oh, no, only like ten minutes."

"Sorry, I just had to make sure I looked good for you," he said quietly, leaning into my ear.

Fifty-year-old men and tacky old ladies in glittery tight pencil skirts kept coming in and out of the entrance. Younger people with foolishly woven cowboy hats loudly chattered and smoked beside us. The atmosphere was like a painting that came directly out of a Spaghetti Western film. The air smelled like Jack Daniel's Tennessee Whiskey, cigarettes and horse shit. I felt happy, and overall tranquil, and comfortable. It almost felt like no one was watching us. Everybody was too drunk to even care.

"You look good," I whispered back at him.

"If I could kiss you right now, I would," he leaned even closer.

"What's stopping you?"

He laughed and winked at me and started to walk towards the entrance. "Come on, let's go get a drink!"

I followed him.

'Johnny B's Outlaw Saloon' was loud and clamorous. White republican men screamed and howled whilst they spilled beer from their beer steins onto the floor. The placed smelled like tobacco and malted liquor. It was rustically elegant and vulgarly charming. The panelled wooden walls and stilted floors gave it a homelike and cosy feeling. The light was dim and obscure. It was the perfect setting for a clandestine romantic meeting like the one Axel and I were about to have. All the way in the back of the saloon, people crowded and gathered in heaps. They were screaming and laughing. And above all the crowd, there was a man in a cowboy hat riding a mechanical bull. The mechanical bull was the star of the show. The mechanical bull was what made 'Johnny B's Outlaw Saloon', **'THE JOHNNY B'S OUTLAW SALOON'.** Everyone in this town wanted to go on it. He was rough. And he was fierce. And the person that could last the longest on it without falling would get a free beer from the house. But no one, of course, could last on top of him for more than ten seconds.

"What do you want?" Axel asked, taking me off guard. I was too distracted by the western bull party that was unfolding in the distance.

"Oh-sorry."

"Don't worry we'll go on that later." He winked at me.

"Oh, are you going to get me drink?"

"Of course, I'm not going to let you pay for it." He masculinely projected his chest towards the ceiling in a dramatic and theatrical manner.

"Well… Thank you…" I smiled, "I think I'll have a Budweiser."

"A Budweiser?" he asked, raising his left eyebrow.

"What's wrong with that?" I laughed.

"Interesting choice."

"It's the one I like," I said.

"Okay," he clumsily rolled his eyes backwards. "Go find us a table," he sensually patted my lower back.

I sat on a rectangular table all the way on the left side of the saloon, far away from the crowds and the mechanical bull. I leaned on the table and observed him whilst he ordered our drinks in the bar. *'How is this real?'*, *'How is this man real?'* His silhouette was refined, but unpolished. The way he moved his arms captivated me, and the way he tucked his long strands of hair behind his ear unbearably twisted the insides of my body. The way he flirted with the female bartender in such a gentle and charming manner made me clench the sides of my chair with fervent ardour. I could feel the power he was going to have over me. I could see my submissiveness and passivity excelling with his superiority and dominance. Watching Axel lean his body on the bar counter whilst he flirted and ordered our drinks, was the same type of feeling I would experience when Jimmy used to choke me and violently fuck me in 'La Santa Espina' motel.

Axel walked towards the table.

"Here you go," Axel handed me a Budweiser.

"What did you get?" I asked, whilst I sipped my beer.

"I got a double whiskey on the rocks," Axel sat on the table. His face right in front of mine. "For this special occasion."

"Special occasion?" I choked on my drink.

"Oh, yes, Mister," he carefully sipped his whiskey, "there is something different about you."

"You are a romantic, aren't you?"

"And so are you."

I chuckled. "Yes… Yes, I am."

"How long have you been here for?"

"Here? Corpus Christi?"

"Yeah."

"I've been here all my life. I grew up here."

"Oh, how come I've never seen you?"

"You already asked me that before…"

"Really…?"

"I think so… ha-ha…"

"To be fair, I *am* older than you… So maybe that's why I haven't seen you about."

"I mean you are only three years older —"

"That's true," he sipped his whiskey once again, "ahhh, this is good!"

"Can I try?"

"Yeah, sure," he handed me his tumbler.

I sipped it cautiously. I gagged. "Oh… Fuck!… Its strong!"

He took the glass from my hands. "Just how I like it." He winked at me. He loved winking at me.

"So… Do you study somewhere or? —"

"I go to college in Arizona… Phoenix."

"Oh-cool… So, I guess you are just here for the summer?"

"Yes… Unfortunately."

"Unfortunately?" he asked, cross-examining me. He could see right through me. He could tell that this town had been the main antagonist in my life.

"Well, you know how parents are. I don't really like my mother. She's kind of a dick," I uncomfortably looked down at the table.

He laughed and tried to go back to our previous subject. "What's your major on?"

"Journalism."

"Oh cool, do you write *poetic* articles then?" he looked at me directly in the eyes, "Was that what you were writing in the pool?"

I wheezed and nodded.

"I mean yeah… I could tell. That pen never left your fingers," he kept looking at me, leaning closer and closer to my face.

I looked towards my left, trying to avoid eye contact. It was too intense. And too soon. This was not the accessible toilet in the locker rooms of the pool. We were in public. And it made me nervous.

"I really want to kiss you right now," he smirked.

I chuckled and went against my primal interior feelings. "Then do it."

"No… I like this game."

"What game?"

"This waiting game—"

"Do you study?" I diffidently tried to break the tactile sexual tension between us.

"What a way to change the conversation… No, I don't. I've only ever worked."

"So, is this the first time you are taking out a man, in let's say 'a romantic way'?" I changed the topic once again.

"Maybe… I mean—" He looked back, trying to see if there was anyone he knew around. "I've always had sexual tension with all my male friends. I'm just a horny man," he whispered.

"I know," I blew him a little subtle kiss.

He stood silent. He took a sip from his whiskey and downed the entirety of it. He loudly sighed. "When do you go back to college?"

"End of August," I grunted and rolled my eyes.

He stayed silent. And looked towards his side. He pondered for a second. "I mean we still have time."

"Yes… I guess we do."

"I want to spend every minute, hour, and day with you until the end of this summer."

"You are not drunk, are you?" I looked at him warily. Men would always say that kind of bullshit inebriated and then forget that you even existed the next morning. I couldn't believe my ears. It was the boldest thing I had heard from a man in a long time, and the worst part of it was that it seemed to come from a genuine and sincere place.

"Oh please… I've just had a double shot of whiskey… I'm a heavyweight… I meant everything I said," he grabbed me by the hand, "come on, let's go dance!" He took me to the dancefloor were a group of loud Texan intoxicated people ferally danced.

Sweet, blonde American couples danced on the wooden floorboards. Men loudly tapped the floor with their cowboy boots. The chandeliers above us swayed back and forth. Axel and I clumsily danced. We both let our bodies loose, letting the music dictate our movements. He spun me around with his left hand. And I almost tripped. I spun him with my right hand after. We looked like best friends. No one suspected anything. For once in my lifetime, I could be whoever I wanted. No one cared about us. Everybody was too busy dancing with their American lovers. I could feel the brassy and vibrant acoustic guitar strums in my chest. I moved to the rhythm of the crowd, and intrinsically let my body unwind. This was what happy western cowboy dreams were made of. There was no judgement. There was no violence. It was just people dancing, laughing and having a good time. And for a second, I forgot that I was with Axel. I closed my eyes and took that exact moment in. *To live life is to live in the present.*

After a few moments, Axel and I realised that people were too drunk to gauge the fact that we were engaging in a homoerotic dance. So, he grabbed me from the back and quickly kissed me on the lips. I blunderingly slapped him. We both laughed. If Mother would have ever seen that, she would've probably had a stroke and a heart attack. But Mother wasn't here. And suddenly, nothing else mattered. Axel was the only person I had on my mind.

Axel and I were taking some fresh air outside the bar at about 11:30PM. We were both smoking his Marlboro red cigarettes. I could see the sweat dripping from his forehead and the wet marks on his back. Although it was night-time, it was excruciatingly hot, and we had danced for a long while. I didn't know why the fuck Axel was wearing a black turtleneck.

"You are good dancer, aren't you?" I sensually patted his sweaty lower back.

"Hahaha, so are you."

"I try, I try," I took a hit from my cigarette, "aren't you hot wearing that?"

"Only a little bit…"

"Why the fuck are you wearing it then?"

"It was the only nice thing in my closet…"

"Well… It's really nice. It suits you very well," I said, with a certain tone of sarcasm in my voice.

"Thank you," he happily breathed out the tobacco smoke from his cigarette.

We both looked at the crowded, bustling parking lot. There was something in the air in Texas every August. People were happy. People were just content to be alive. And you could see that by the drunk people that cheerfully laughed and danced as they walked out of the establishment. The drunk American ladies holding their high heels, who walked bare feet on the cemented pavement. And the drunk gentlemen that hugged and kissed their male friends. They had all just had the best night of their lives.

"That moment... When I kissed you in the middle of the dancefloor... That was something I've never experienced," Axel stealthily uttered.

"I enjoyed it," I looked back at him. I wanted him to hug me so bad.

"Want to come back to mine tonight?"

I stood silent, not knowing what to say.

"You can say no—"

"I would love to..." I loudly sighed, "I'm just thinking about my mother."

"Oh, I see..."

But then it just hit me like a spark. "I could sneak you into my room though." That was an even worse idea, but I was willing to risk everything. I didn't want Mother to take more away from me.

"Oh yeah?"

"Yeahhh!"

"Are you sure?"

I pondered for a second and thought about Mother. *'Fuck it.'* "Yes... I'm sure."

"Sounds good, then." He kissed me on the lips. "I'll make sure to not make you scream tonight."

I squinted and hugged him.

"Okay but before we go. We need to go try the mechanical bull out!" he enthusiastically suggested.

"Yes, let's go!"

This love was already starting to intoxicate me.

I had never ridden a mechanical bull ever in my life before. But there is a first time for everything. And just like I threw myself into the unknown void of Axel, I threw myself onto the bull with no expectations. I gripped the red strap tightly that draped on the side of the bull's head and promised myself that I was going to win that free beer. The man that manoeuvred the robotic machine pressed a button. The bull started to sway side by side slowly. My whole body trembled to the movement of the bull.

"You got this!" Axel shouted from the outside of the ring.

I smiled back at him. The bull had already started to shake more and more aggressively. It became harder to grip onto the red strap with every second. But I tried. I really tried. My body and bones started to twitch and quiver as the bull savagely moved back and forth. Like a lightning bolt, the bull started to move faster and faster. It was impossible to grasp onto the red strap. The bull was shaking and tossing me like a crocodile attacking an antelope in the African Savanna. The mechanical bull moved up and down ferociously and made my body brutally fall onto the inflated cushioned floor. Everyone laughed and clapped. I stood up and brushed the dust from my ass off. I walked up to Axel.

"Well done," he gently smacked my ass.

"Thank you," I giggled. I felt embarrassed. "It's harder than it looks."

"My turn," he tossed his blue denim-pinned jacket onto my chest.

Axel went on top of the bull like a macho man. He flexed his arms and put his tongue out. Axel was an unrefined raunchy clown. I liked his humour. He traced me a heart with his fingers on the air. He wanted to make a fool of himself. He wanted to make me laugh. I liked men that didn't take themselves that seriously. And Axel was great at doing that. He knew he was gorgeous. But he also knew that he had to be humble about it. And I loved that.

I tightly pressed his denim jacket against my chest and

tenderly sniffed it. It smelled like most of my wet dreams. Notes of smoky wood, frankincense and a touch of manly armpit sweat.

The guy pressed the button and the bull started to move. Axel clutched the red strap firmly. I could tell that he wanted to impress me. The bull quivered brusquely, and Axel's body trembled and shook to the rhythm of it. I knew why Axel wanted to go on the bull. Axel looked like he was fucking the bull. He wanted to show me how he was going to fuck the shit out of me later that night. The bull started to rattle and shudder in such a truculent and aggressive manner. But Axel was determined. He wasn't going to fall right away. His veiny arms grasped the red strap tightly. The bull shook his body side by side. He strongly grabbed the bull's back. He wanted to flaunt his strength and muscles. But not even a Greek God could beat this bull. Axel fell right down to the floor. I laughed and clapped. Everyone else did the same. Axel stood up and fixed his hair. He tucked the strands of his caramel hazel hair behind his ears. He looked rather upset and disappointed. A man that had just been emasculated.

"Good job," I said, handing him his denim jacket back.

"Better than you, for sure," he teased me, petting my head in a playful manner.

"Okay, let's not get too cocky," I jokingly countered.

"You are only starting to get to know me..." He put his denim jacket on.

"You looked hot."

"I know."

"Shall we go?" I asked.

"To your house?" he chuckled and looked into my eyes. He knew exactly what I was expecting from him after I had seen him ride the bull that way.

"Yes..."

He bit his lower lip and tapped my lower back. "Let's go then!"

We both joyously walked towards the entrance of the saloon with a few drinks in our blood stream and a new-found love in our pockets.

We both nervously stood in the front porch of my house.

"Shhhhhhh! You must be quiet!" I whispered.

"Yes. Don't worry," he murmured back. I could tell that he was slightly apprehensive and nervous.

I opened the door of my house. All the lights were off. It was pitch-black and you could barely see a thing. My heart was hardly beating. This had to be one of the riskiest things I had ever done in my life. If Mother were ever to find out, she would hang me and send me to hell. But thankfully, both Mother and Father were asleep. And both Mario and Quique were away. I grabbed Axel by the hand and took him through the staircase all the way up to my room, making sure we didn't make too much noise. Luckily, my room was on the third floor of the house, isolated from everything else, like Cinderella's room in her stepmother's house. Thank fuck my parents' room was located on the ground floor. I quietly opened the door of my room and let Axel in. I closed it quickly right after.

Axel pinned me against the wall and savagely kissed me. I had been waiting for this moment all night long. He grabbed my arms and hands and clutched them together with his left muscly arm. He feasted on my neck as I gripped his long greasy hair tightly. We were both volatile and mercurial. I took my shirt off and he took his. He picked me up from my legs and carried me towards my whitewashed cotton linen bed. He threw me on the mattress and shredded my bootcut jeans apart. This was love. This was unpredictable love. I had never been touched that way before. Not even Jimmy had ever touched me like that. The way he looked at me whilst he touched me was so virtuous and pure that it almost felt like we weren't doing something sinful and unholy. He took his jeans off and thrusted me with his mint green Ralph Lauren boxers on. The erections underneath our boxers throbbed against each other. I wrapped my hairy legs around his back and grasped his cheeks with my feisty hands.

"Fuck me," I whispered on his ears as he dry humped me harder and harder.

"Oh yeah?"

"Fuck me as hard as you can."

"I don't want to make you scream, baby."

"Do it!" I commanded, rapidly dashing my geometrical patterned boxers off.

He threw his mint green Ralph Lauren boxers across the room and bedazzled me with his voluptuous erection. He spat on his hand and stroked his dick back and forth. He grabbed his cock and slipped it right inside my anus. I grasped the back of his head belligerently and pushed his forehead against mine. I moaned. I moaned really loud. There was no better feeling than his dick inside of me. He grunted. His whiskey tobacco-filled breath all over my face. I closed my eyes and thought about the way Axel's body trembled when he was on top of the mechanical bull. He no longer was fucking the bull. He was fucking *me*. I opened my eyes. And looked at him directly into the irises of his eyes. *'The end of this summer was going to be like riding a mechanical bull.'*

VII

Axel (Interlude)

Revelation 12:9

"The great dragon was hurled down
- that ancient serpent called the devil,
or Satan, who leads the whole world astray.
He was hurled to the earth,
and his angels with him."

It was the fourth of August 1996 and I had woken up at 6AM completely dumbfounded. Brutally thunderstruck. Axel was sleeping beside me, resting his cheeks on my left pillow, snoring and drooling into the white cotton sheets. He almost ran a marathon last night fucking me. His body was probably extremely exhausted and drained from that cardio. I went on my side and looked at him. He looked beautiful whilst sleeping. I caressed his cheeks with my fingers, valuing the sensation his prickly stubble caused on my fingertips. I traced his lips with my thumb. I then placed my left hand on his hairy chest. I could feel his heartbeat. The way his heart pulsated on the palm of my hand exposed his love for me. He had fallen in love. And I had too. This man was going to become the thief of my own heart. I rested my hand on his chest and wrapped myself under his body. I gripped on his muscly veiny arms and tried to fall asleep again.

'How did this all come into fruition?' Only a few days ago, I was tucked inside my own bed reminiscing about the time when Jimmy used to fuck me in 'La Santa Espina' motel. And only a day ago, I was daydreaming about what it would be like to suddenly find love. What it would be like to have a man wrapped around my body in my own bed. And then here was Axel beside

99

me, with his arms all over my deceased corpse. It was all starting to feel like a fever dream which was hard to gauge. *'Did I want to fall in love again?', 'Was this just a farce?', 'What if this was just going to be a one-night stand?'* I leaned in and gave Axel a kiss on the cheeks. He was still deeply asleep.

Axel was sleeping in my own bed. Axel was underneath the rooftop of my own house. I looked up at the ceiling and pondered for a second. My heart started to race, and my forehead started to sweat. Axel had to leave before Mother would wake up. But I didn't want this moment to end so abruptly. It was so beautiful. Magical. Whimsical. Mother had already taken a lot away from my life already. *'Fuck Mother.'* I wasn't going to let her take this moment away from me. I wasn't going to jeopardize this moment for Mother's sake.

So, I decided that I was just going to wait for Mother and Father to wake up and leave the house before I'd step out of my bedroom with Axel. Although I tried to enjoy the moment, the anxiety was still there. Mother could come upstairs at any given time and knock the door of my room. But I was willing to take that risk. I could already feel that I was going to take so many risks for Axel. And that was scary. Because men are scary. You never know what their true intentions are. One day they treat you like you are one of the most beautiful people they have ever laid their eyes on, and then the next day, they decide they no longer want to see you ever again. I could already feel myself catching feelings for someone I had only met a day ago. This was dangerous. I was starting to play with fire again. *'Had I not learnt my lessons with Jimmy?', 'Why did I like to put myself in these situations?'* The last time I played with fire I got cruelly burnt to death.

I could already feel Axel's axe stabbed on my shoulder. He had already imprinted me. There was no going back. I had already given him my body. And if Axel were ever to abandon me like Jimmy did, I was never going to be able to truly recover in my life. I've always thought that if you're ever afraid of losing someone, and that anxiety consumes your whole body after you've been fucked in the ass by them for the first time, then that means they're not meant for you. My head started to spin. My body started to tremble. I was starting to feel dizzy and nauseous. I was scared for my life. I was afraid of the character that Axel was going to play in my life. I had lost all of my trust in men, and if my heart were to ever break again, the only way I could be able to piece myself back together would be through my own ultimate death.

He opened his eyes and looked at me. I could see it in his irises. This wasn't going to end pretty. This man was going to finally take my life away. This man was going to take my integrity away. This man was going to make me do stuff I had never ever done in my life before. I could see our destiny. I could see my *own* destiny. I was going to start walking bare feet on broken glass. He touched my left cheek with his right hand. He leaned in for a kiss. His lips were scorching warm. It was a kiss sent directly from hell. He inserted his tongue inside my mouth. I could taste the lies, the manipulation, the villain he was going to turn me into. And he could taste my susceptibility, my vulnerability, and my weakness. He could tell that my bones had already been broken, and that the insides of my body had already been left rotting by the men that had scorned me. He kissed me harder with fervent passion. It wasn't a kiss out of love. It was a tyrant, fascist kiss. Like the doomed fate a corrupt prophet shows you in a magical crystal ball, I could see things were going to take a very dark turn. But I wanted him to hurt me. I wanted him to take the small amount of power I had inside of me away. I wanted him to destroy me. I was bored, and my life had become immensely monotonous. I needed that pain. I needed those hands heartlessly gripping my neck.

This was the summer I was going to become a fallen angel. This was the summer Mother, Father, God, Jesus and the citizens of this town were going to expel me from the gates of their heavens. Like Satan, I was going to fall from the sky onto the scorching fiery flames of hell. Because I have had enough of the abuse. I have had enough of the maltreatment. If God allowed Father Orlando and Hunter to viciously rape me, then I was going to show God what I was able to do with my own hands. Axel was going to be the person that was going to unleash the hungry, feisty beast inside of me these abusive and slanderous men had created. Axel was going to be the vessel and catalyst of my rise against these hypocritical corrupt authorities.

I was done being naive and gullible. I didn't want to be loved anymore. I didn't want to be cared for anymore. Mother had already rejected me my entire life. And God had already abandoned me since the day I was born. I wasn't the boy that got raped at fifteen anymore. I had already gained experience and knowledge. Villains weren't born villains, and antagonists weren't born antagonists. Villains were misunderstood people who rebelled and rioted against the abuse they had endured in the past. And that is why I had always secretly related to the Devil. Like the antagonists in Greek tragedies, I woke up that morning beside Axel and decided it was all going to change. I was no longer going to allow men to hurt me. I was no longer going to fall for a man's 'I love you.' I was going to become the church's worst nightmare. I was going to rebel against the society that had wronged me. I was going to show everybody what resuscitating from the dead looked like. I was going to make Mother, Father Orlando, and Hunter pay for their deceitful and fraudulent degeneracies in the name of Satan. *'Oh hail, Satan!'*

If Jimmy was an angel sent to me from heaven, Axel was a demon sent to me from hell. Demons had the big, monstrous and beastly penises I liked. I could feel the demonic possession travelling through my bloodstream. I had already been possessed. I had already been enticed. Satan's war with God had already begun. I had never felt so much rush and thrill in my life before. I had never previously felt so much adrenaline been discharged from my adrenal glands. This wasn't love. This was a pact with the Devil. I sold my body and soul to Satan last night by letting Axel open my ass cheeks and allowing him to fuck the living shit out of me with his thorn-like phallus. Axel and I were going to become the incarnation of revenge. Axel and I were going to sinfully turn all the crosses on the walls of my house upside down. Axel and I were going to mercilessly castrate Fathers and priests and feed the cathedral's gargoyles their mutilated and disremembered testicles. Axel and I were going to become the five-star generals of Satan's flamed army. Axel and I were going to wreck-havoc against the two-faced hypocritical so-called angels. Axel and I were going to burn the bible and expose all of its lies and falsehoods. Axel and I were going to strangle and hang bigoted homophobic nuns with the string of their rosaries.

My past and trauma had been leaking into the present unexpectedly since the beginning of the summer when I came back home. But the time had come to let those accumulated bodies of swamped-rotten water loose. I was ready to open the floodgates and drown everybody with my tsunami.

It was 9AM. I heard some movement coming from downstairs. Mother had probably already woken up and was getting ready to leave the house.

"Good morning," Axel said with his manly low-pitched grungy morning voice after our long make-out kiss.

"Good morning."

"Are you okay?" He knew exactly what I had been pondering about all night long.

"Yes," I lied. I wasn't okay. I had only been enlightened by Satan moments before.

"You sure?"

"Yes," I insisted, grabbing his fingers tightly and brushing them against my coarse juicy lips. We kissed again.

"Wow! Someone's extra horny and feisty today!"

"I like it when you kiss me hard."

"Oh, I know you do," he laughed. He then looked at me again. He examined my body language. "You seem nervous…"

"Mother. I am nervous of Mother," I brusquely responded. I lied again. I was trying to suppress all the thoughts I had been dealing with since 6AM.

"Oh shit. Yeah. Is she going to come up?" Axel quickly put the cotton covers over his naked body.

"I don't think so… She's always got stuff to do in the mornings… She doesn't really give a shit about me."

"Well, that's good."

"Yeah, I guess—"

"Because that means I can have you all for myself." He leaned in for another kiss and grabbed my waistline with his refined ogre-like hands.

"Shhhh! Be quiet!" I howled.

We both remained silent. We looked at the ceiling and held each other's hands tightly. Even though we had only met a day ago, it felt like we had known each other for much longer than that. It felt like we were meant for one another. It felt like I was going to allow him to hold the baton of our future and prospective 'relationship'. It felt like I was going to allow him to dominate and manipulate me. It felt like I was going to allow him to convince me of committing crime.

"What are you doing today?" I asked.

"I have to go lifeguard at 1."

"Oh, cool —"

"Why?"

"Just wondering…" I rested my head on his chest once again and traced and picked on the hairs around his nipples.

"You?"

"I don't know yet."

He was silent and still. He didn't know what to say. We were both feeling the same thing. Our minds were synchronised. He knew exactly what was going on inside my mind. The sunlight that peeked through the shutters of my window into our tangled naked bodies felt warmer and warmer as the tension inside my bedroom increased.

"Axel. I'm scared."

"What do you mean?"

"I don't know. I'm just scared. I'm scared of you."

He laughed and hugged me. "Why are you scared of me?" he asked with a sarcastic tone of voice.

"The power you already have over me," I held his hand tightly, "your hand has already ripped my heart apart."

"Well, what can I say? I am a ten out of a ten."

"I know," I murmured. But Axel didn't know that I had experienced a dark twisted prophesy and predicament earlier that morning.

"I liked fucking you," he smiled, playing with the fat on my cheeks.

"I liked getting fucked by you."

"I liked the fact that you did everything I told you to."

I nervously giggled, not knowing what to say. The morning warmth was starting to warm up my room. The air started to feel humid and stuffy. The thoughts in my mind had probably overpowered the heat that was already burning inside my body.

"I like people that obey."

"And I like to obey," I sensually said, whilst I slowly sucked on his right thumb.

"I like our connection."

"You are really, really, handsome."

"I know," he held my body even tighter. Something specific was on his mind. "Can I ask you a question?"

"Yeah, sure…"

"But promise you won't freak the fuck out?"

"I promise."

"I don't believe you."

"No, no, I promise," I gave him my pinky finger, "pinky promise."

"Okay."

Axel struggled to talk. He started to stumble on his words. He had been dumbfounded and stupefied the same way I had been throughout the night and morning.

"What?" I eagerly asked, wanting to know what he was going to ask me.

He glanced right through me. "Do you want to be my boyfriend?"

My world collided. The roof top above our heads crashed right into us. The fire that was already cooking up inside of me exploded into a forest-fire. No one had ever asked me that before. No one had ever asked me to be their boyfriend ever in my life. But this was fast. This couldn't be real. This felt rushed. This felt wrong. I couldn't say yes. I had only met him yesterday. I didn't know if I could commit to someone who had only showed me one of their facades. This felt like a miracle sent from hell. This had been plotted by Satan. Axel was coming to save me from the corrupt and perverted gates from heaven. I couldn't say no. But I stood quiet. I paralysed. I was unable to speak.

"I knew I shouldn't have asked you that question." I could see the disappointment and embarrassment on his face.

"No, no, it's not that."

"Then what is it?"

"I was just surprised."

"So, you don't want to be my boyfriend?"

"I do."

Axel gasped. "Are you sure?"

"I'd love to be your boyfriend," I smiled. It was the biggest smile I had ever had on my face.

"Okay." He didn't have to rectify my answer again. A yes was a yes. And I had already been tricked into his mousetrap. There was no going back. There is no room for remorse or repent when you make a pact with the Devil. Once you sign the contract and treaty, the only way out is through one's absolute death.

I sealed our fiendish and diabolical agreement with a long-lasting kiss. I knew what I was getting myself into. I didn't sign the contract blindsided. I signed it knowing all the terms and conditions of this partnership. And I was ready to see how this was going to change my life, forever, and ever.

The front door from downstairs loudly slammed. I heard hurried footsteps heading towards the driveway. After a few moments, I heard the car in my driveway take off. Mother and Father were finally gone.

"My parents are gone," I said, whilst I placed his left hand on my rock-hard erection.

"Oh yeah?"

"Yes."

Axel bit his lower lip. "Then turn around and let me fuck you."

I turned around and spread my ass cheeks wide open. He stroked his veiny throbbing penis back and forth until it was stiff enough to slip it right into me. He spat on his hand and spread the saliva-infused lubricant up and down his cock.

"Are you ready?" he asked.

"Yes."

He pierced right through me. One hand on my shoulder. The other one around my neck. Satan fucked me doggy-style.

PART TWO

Isaiah 14:13

"You said in your heart,
I will ascend to the heavens;
I will raise my throne
above the stars of God;
I will sit enthroned on the mount of assembly,
on the utmost heights of Mount Zaphon."

VIII

Sex Tape

2 Timothy 3:4

*"Treacherous, reckless, conceited,
lovers of pleasure rather than lovers of God."*

I had always struggled with my mind. The voices inside my brain were excruciatingly loud and tiresome. They screamed and pierced right through my eardrums. They made my heart skip a beat faster. They made my hands sweat and my vision blur. Anxiety had always consumed my life. I always tended to categorize my days as good or bad merely on the fact of whether I had an anxiety attack or not. I didn't like anxiety. I didn't like to feel uneasy. I didn't like to feel like I wasn't in control of things. I was the worst person in taking things as they came. I was the worst person at 'going with the flow'.

Throughout my life, I had always struggled with my past and the dreading outcome of the future. *What if the thoughts in my head come true?', 'What if I am indeed a prophet, and the conspiracy theories I have created inside my mind materialize into reality?', 'What if God is real and will send me to the gates of hell after my death for all the treasons I've committed?'* These were the type of questions that had been keeping me up at night all my life. These were the type of doubts that would keep me in the verge of having a mental breakdown in my day-to-day basis.

This summer, my anxiety had gotten out of control more than ever in my life. My past kept creeping up on me in such a volatile manner, and it got harder and harder to suppress it every time. Corpus Christi had already taken my happiness and tranquillity away in the past. Returning to this town after my

111

freshman year of college had become the nightmare I thought I had already woken up from. The streets of this town, the crosses and images of Jesus Christ on the shopfronts, the buildings next to the catholic boys' school I used to go, all screamed one name. And that name was: Father Orlando.

It was the eighteenth of August 1996, and it had been two weeks since Axel and I had first had sex and had fallen in love with each other. Axel magically appeared in my life out of nowhere. And the love and infatuation I had for him was uncontrollable. Axel was confident, nonchalant, careless and reckless. I had no control over him. I had no control over the power he had over me. And that scared me. I thought he was only going to be a one-night stand. But I was wrong. Extremely, annoyingly wrong. Axel wanted me. And not just for one night. He wanted me for the rest of his summer. I had always wanted to feel 'wanted.' And Axel really wanted me. He was controlling and manipulative. And I was compliant and acquiescent.

We had fucked more than three times every day since our first night. In the last two weeks our record for most fucks in a day had been six. We were both torturously attracted to each other. And our power dynamic was extremely palatable and compatible. He wanted to be dominant and commanding, and I wanted to be subordinate and submissive. Axel had an enormous dick with big swollen-up testicles that would lovingly bounce back and forth on my perineum whenever he would brutally drill me. Axel was impulsive and adventurous. And I was crazy and obedient. Our relationship was mostly based around sex and exploring the boundaries of our own body. Axel and I got addicted to the pleasure and dopamine of lovemaking. Like a heroin addict, I couldn't live without his cum in my mouth and his cock inside my ass for more than two hours. We were both living in a hedonistic and nymphomaniac fever dream.

Having sex in my bedroom became extremely boring and monotonous after our first three days. The stakes were excruciatingly low, and the threats we faced at that time weren't as menacing anymore. The threat of Mother walking in on us dissipated within a few days, and no longer made us horny.

Axel and I decided that this summer was going to become our summer of spitefulness and naughtiness. My anxiety and overpowering thoughts had to be relieved by something. And that something was sex. The act of penetration and sucking dick rapidly became conventional. There had to be something more. Something that would make us feel ungodly and immoral. Something that would make us feel disgusting and repugnant. Corpus Christi had suddenly become our lawless land. There were suddenly no more rules. There was just non-stop sex and pleasure.

The first two weeks of our relationship became a hedonistic paradise. All I wanted to do was to soak the sun in. I wanted to drink, I wanted to smoke weed, I wanted to feel loved, and I wanted to get fucked in the ass hard. I had magically forgotten about all my troubles. They had magically disappeared into the back drawer of my brain. Dick and weed became my anaesthesia. And I didn't want anything more. This was when our summer truly began. When we both stopped giving a fuck.

'Summer of '69' by Bryan Adams became our national anthem. And Axel would play it as loud as his cherry-red Jetta could whilst we drove in the highway past the speed limits. We would drive into downtown baked and high. There was no better feeling than putting my head out of the window when Axel would drive us through the freeway next to the sea. The smell of the ocean and the beautiful midnight blue of the Gulf of Mexico would exacerbate the level of my marijuana highness.

$$***$$

Axel and I would sneak out of our houses in the middle of the night and would drive to the sand dunes in the north part of 'Nueces Bay' to hold our hands and observe the stars together. But mostly to have sex on the sand under the stars and constellations.

Sneaking out of our houses at the dead of night became our

tradition. And we would find thrilling, new exciting places to fuck every night. On the Sunday of our one-week anniversary of our relationship, I let him piss on my bare naked chest in Rose Hill Memorial Park at 2AM. Our relationship had no boundaries. We were both kinky and horny. The smell of his clear, translucent urine that came out of the urethral meatus of his penis filled my body with ecstatic pride and joy. I wanted to worship everything that came out of his body.

"Can I aim inside your mouth?" he asked, whilst he pissed on my chest.

"Yes." I grabbed his cock and put it inside my mouth. His summer sweaty hairy pubes were all over my eyes and face. He pissed inside my mouth. And I swallowed it. My mouth rousingly caught on fire. He liked to degrade me. He liked to humiliate me. And I liked it too.

"You are my little bitch," he wiped the urine off the corners of my lips with the tip of his penis.

$$***$$

Axel and I once broke into the Salvador Perez Public Swimming Pool to go for a late-night swim at 4AM. We were both young and free and liked to break every single rule that ever existed.

"Strip for me," he whispered. We were both standing at the edge of the pool with sweaty humid clothes on.

"Are we skinny dipping?" I started to unbutton my Carhartt red-black-white patterned short sleeve shirt.

"Of course!" Axel quickly stripped his jeans off. He tore his tight black ribbed tank top apart. He threw his boxers towards the nearest sunbed. His soft penis and testicles hung and dangled all the way to the floor. He jumped into the pool. "Come on!"

I tossed my short sleeve shirt and black denim bootcuts onto the sunbed. I slowly started to take my boxers off. I was trying to tease Axel.

"Oh, come on, you idiot!" He splashed me a tsunami with pool water.

I took my boxers off. I covered my erection and balls with my hands and jumped into the pool.

Axel quickly swam to me. He took the back of my head and kissed me. We shared a long French kiss. His tongue tasted like bleach and chlorine.

"I love you," Axel uttered, spitting pool water out of his mouth.

I gasped and remained silent. No one had ever said that to me. I didn't know how to respond to that.

He kissed my forehead. "Aren't you going to say, 'I love you' back?" he dashed my wet hair back and forth.

"Fuck me first," I smiled back at him.

"Here… inside the pool?"

"Yes," I pushed his face towards mine.

Axel fucked me as hard as he could inside the pool.

***

Shoplifting became our newfound hobby. There was no better cocaine rush than bending the rules. We would drive up to our local Walmart and walk out with Coke bottles and Doritos bags inside our hoodies, just for the pure sake of fucking with the authorities. And because stealing was fun. Axel quit his job two days after meeting me. He wanted to seize the moment and spend most of his time with me. We had no money, but that wasn't a problem because I would steal twenty-dollar bills from Father's wallet at night. We were both going off the rails. Our hedonistic and self-indulgent lifestyle had gotten out of control. But I was living the life I had always wanted to live. And nothing mattered more in life than the things Axel and I did together.

***

Thrifting clothes had always been my biggest passion. I had always liked clothes. And Axel worshipped clothes the same way I did. Axel had always had his own sense of style; he was naturally cool and majestically aesthetic. I, on the other hand, had to try really hard to be 'cool'. Johnny Ramone was my idol and I wanted to dress, and look like him. But I never truly succeeded.

However, at the same time, I wanted to change my identity. I wanted to change my whole self. I wanted to buy new clothes. I wanted a fresh start. But most importantly I wanted to be as cool as Axel. So 'Goodwill Thrift' became our number one provider in fashion, because it was the cheapest and easiest to steal from.

We were both browsing the clothing rack that was all the way in the back of the store. Tacky white, fluorescent lights shone brightly above us. Raunchy country music played in the background. All the clothes smelled like musty onion and out of date garlic.

"You like this one?" Axel showed me a black washed-out Metallica tee.

"Eh… It's kind of basic."

He rolled his eyes and put it back.

"How about this one?" he showed me a grey tie-dye Ramones tee.

I quickly snatched it out of his hands. "This one is for *me*," I chuckled and walked towards the jeans section.

He rolled his eyes once again.

After a few moments of browsing, I went up to Axel with more than thirteen items on my arms.

"Holy fuck!" he sighed, "Are those leopard print fur coats for us?"

"I just want to see how they look on us."

"We are going to look like pimps."

"So what?" I walked towards the fitting room, and he followed me.

We both entered the same fitting room. 'Goodwill Thrift' was always short in staff, and the little number of staff they had were dumb seventy-year-old volunteers that would sit on the desk all the way in the front of the store and stare at the glitchy television above them. There was no one outside the fitting rooms to count our items. I dropped the fur coats, the denim jeans, and the other ten tees on the plastic chair in front of the mirror.

"Come on! Let's try the fur coats on!" I childishly jumped back and forth.

"Okay…" Axel responded in a passionless manner.

I put my coat on and handed him his. He put it on. They were both oversized and smelled like musty cat urine. We both looked in the mirror and laughed. We both indeed looked like pimps from the seventies. Suddenly Axel's mood had changed. I could feel the shift of energy. Axel looked at me through the mirror deeply and slowly started to caress the bulge underneath his denims. He bit his lower lip.

"How horny are you?" he asked me.

"Why?" I chuckled.

"What if I told you I wanted to fuck you right here?"

"Here?" I loudly laughed.

"Yes… Here…"

I pondered for a second. This was going to be memorable and iconic. This was going to become a huge milestone in our relationship and sexual life. I had to say yes. So, I grabbed him from the neck and harshly kissed his lips. We made out with both of our leopard print fur coats on. We were two leopards devouring each other. There was no time to waste. He pulled his jeans and underwear down. His jeans and boxers were tangled between his legs and ankles. He took his cock out and savagely pulled my pants down. I put my hands on the mirror and arched my back. He spat on his hand and lubricated my asshole with his saliva. He put his penis inside of me and fucked the shit out of me. It was hot and sweaty, and everything got sticky really quick. Both of us still had our leopard print fur coats on whilst fucking. I fearlessly moaned. Axel put his hand over my mouth. He was trying to silence me. Axel came inside my ass in a matter of seconds. This was the biggest risk we had ever taken together. There was no better feeling than the thrill and terror you would feel inside your body when fucking in a public space. We were both exploring our primitive and barbarian roots. And breaking every fucking damn rule.

We both walked out of the fitting room with three stolen T-shirts each, hidden underneath our zip up hoodies. We were both sweaty and red, as if we had just come out of a sauna. We walked all the way to the front of the store as fast as we could, avoiding eye contact with all the other customers. We walked out of the automatic doors of the shop into the hot-scorching parking lot. The sun was jolly bright. And life was better than ever before. I was happy. Or at least that is what I thought. The swamped-rotten water still brimmed the floodgates.

Axel and I were both out of our minds. We had no values and morals left. We walked towards his cherry-red Jetta. We sat inside his car and uncontrollably laughed for hours.

"Give me a high five!"

I gave him the hardest high five he had ever received from anyone in his life.

He turned the engine on and drove off the strip mall's parking lot.

✳✳✳

It was the evening of the eighteenth of August. I was lying on Axel's sweaty and prickly chest in his room after we had fucked.

The sun was starting to set. And the breeze that came from the window beautifully pushed the white linen curtains into the air. Axel and I were madly in love. We had been fucking non-stop for two weeks straight. But like a cruel and vicious drug, there was just never enough. There was something we hadn't done before. There was still something left on the back of the drawer.

"Can I ask you something weird...?" Axel asked. He looked down at me with a serious face.

"What... now?" I cackled.

"I've been thinking for a while... there is something I've always wanted to do. But my ex-girlfriend never wanted to do it. But I've always had this craving of doing it—"

"What is it?" I desperately shrieked.

"I don't know – it's kind of weird."

"I mean you've already pissed on me... Don't tell me you want to shit on me now—"

"No, no, no, I would never do that. That is disgusting."

"You wanted to *shit on me*?" I laughed.

"No!" he laughed with me. He was embarrassed. He put his hand on his face.

"You are now lying to me... because I looked at you with utter disgust."

"No, no, I promise it wasn't that."

"Then, what is it?"

"Well, I have this Sony camcorder my father gave me for Christmas..."

"Uh-huh?"

"And I wanted to see if you wanted to film a sex tape?"

I felt like a hole was being perforated into my heart. *What level of insanity and madness had we reached?'* I didn't know what to say. My face stayed blank. *'Why did he want to film a sex tape?', 'Who was he going to show it to?', 'What if someone ever saw it somewhere?'*

"You can say no," he said with a certain quality of disappointment and dismay on his face.

"Why do you want to do it?" I threw an arrow across his heart.

"I don't know. It's kind of hot, I guess."

"Who are you going to show it to?"

"No one… it's for us."

I felt the pressure. I didn't want to argue. We had never had an argument before. I just wanted to please him. I just wanted to appease him. I just wanted to do whatever *he* wanted to do. I looked at him directly in the eyes. "You promise you won't show it to anyone…?"

"Promise… it's only for us," he handed me his pinky finger.

"Okay, let's do it," I quietly mumbled.

We had lived in a lawless land for far too long. Boundaries had disappeared into thin air. Nothing was ever enough. We were never able to be fully satisfied. We were always hungry for more. We were both doomed by the ultimate curse of hedonism.

Axel took his old-school mini-DV Sony TRV-900e camcorder and placed it on the desk in front of his bed. The lights of his bedroom were brightly seductive. It was already dark outside. I was on his bed naked on all fours. Axel clicked the 'REC' button and walked towards the bed. A blinking red light shone above the lens of the camcorder. Axel stroked his cock back and forth. He knelt on the bed, spun me around and pushed my head towards his cock. He was brutal and aggressive. More than ever before. Everything felt performative and artificial. He was used to me obeying him. But I didn't want to obey him at that moment. He wanted to abuse me in front of the camera. He callously crammed his penis inside of my mouth, making me cry and brutishly gag. This didn't feel like love anymore. This felt like something similar I had experienced before in this same town. My heart started to thump off-beat, and my ears started to piercingly ring. I didn't want to do this. But I had already said yes. I could feel the anticipation of an anxiety attack striking inside my body. I closed my eyes and tried to think of something else. The thing I always used to do when men would abuse me. Axel loved me. He was doing this because he loved me. And I was doing this because I loved him. I was doing this because I didn't want to disappoint or upset him. He moaned out of pleasure. He was thoroughly enjoying this. But I wasn't. Whilst he was getting pleasure out of it, I was getting tortured. He made this about himself. I no longer was part of the equation. The only thing that kept me going was the fact that I knew that this gave him pleasure and made him happy. And my only mission in my life was to please the people I loved.

"Stop!" He pulled his cock out of my mouth. "You are going to make me cum!!!" he laughed, "Turn around!"

I turned around and went down on all fours. I arched my back. He spat on his hand and fingered my hole. He was trying to loosen me up. He drilled his rock-hard penis inside of me back and forth. But this time, it hurt. It really hurt. He put his left hand on my shoulder and pulled my hair with his right hand. He growled and groaned like an animal every time he pounded my ass. He was putting on a performance for the camera.

"Do you want me to cum inside of you?"

I moaned out of fright and pain. This was bringing me back to that moment. The moment I had been trying to suppress for the entirety of my life.

"I said, do you want me to cum inside of you?" He slapped my face with fervent violence.

Axel's words went in one ear and out the other. I couldn't stop thinking about Father Orlando.

"Ugh, baby you are going to make me cum," he rolled his eyes and loudly howled. He pierced his penis deep inside my rectum. As deep as my anus allowed it. I shut my eyes tight and reminded myself that Axel loved me. And I loved Axel. This wasn't abuse. This was love. I looked up at the camera. The red light above the lens kept blinking. All of my suffering and distress had been captured on camera.

Axel came inside of me. He loudly sighed. He rested his face on the back of my head and stayed silent for a minute. He was catching his breath. He took his cock out of my ass.

He kissed my left cheek with his dry coarse salty lips. "I'm going to love you forever."

"No, you are not," I timidly looked down at the wrinkled covers of the bed, trying to conceal my tears. My heart kept pulsating.

"I'll be the last person you'll see before you die on your death bed." Axel stood up from the bed, grabbed the camera and clicked the 'STOP' button. The camera stopped recording.

Axel was no longer just going to be a memory in the back of my head. A tape with our so-called love caught on camera was now actually existent. Ready to be found and discovered. And one day, someone was going to find it like the oxidized Edwardian jewellery they found inside the shipwrecked Titanic deep down in the ocean.

IX

Holy Cross of San Lorenzo Catholic Boys School

Matthew 4:8-9

"Again, the devil took him to a very high mountain
and showed him all the kingdoms of the world
and their splendour.
'All this I will give you,' he said,
'If you will bow down and worship me.'"

It was dusk on the nineteenth of August 1996, and I was lying on Axel's chest in his bedroom once again. We were both dressed. He was wearing a tight red tee that had a sunshine cartoon with sunglasses in the middle of it. His baggy denim shorts exposed his masculine hairy legs. He smelled like sweat, but I liked it. I enjoyed resting my head near his armpits. I would sometimes take a deep sniff on them. I liked how my man smelled. It was the smell of a hot scorching Texan summer. I was wearing a white ribbed tank top and a pair of electric blue athletic running shorts. I had just gone for a run around the neighbourhood before coming to Axel's house.

He was playing with my hair. We were both silent, trying to take every moment in. We only had a week and a half left before I had to go back to Arizona to start my sophomore year in college. We were both sad. But we never talked about it. It was about 8PM and the sun was setting. The breeze that came from Axel's window aired our sweaty legs out. Even though it was warm and sticky, we were both unable to unstick from each other. I always wanted to be all over his body. And he never wanted our legs to stop twisting one another. We were always horny. The erections that protruded through our shorts always exposed our lustful libido.

"How was your run?" he ran his fingers on my long greasy fringe.

"It was good. I felt like I was going to pass out – it was so hot. But I powered through."

"Well done," he gave me a wet kiss on my forehead.

"How was your day?"

"My day was good – slightly boring without you."

"Well, I'm here now," my hand travelled from his thorax towards the erection in his baggy denim shorts. I started to throb his boner back and forth.

"Oh, yeah?"

"Yeah," I smiled and blushed.

"You know what we should do?" he said, biting his lower lip.

"What?"

"We should jack off to our sex tape."

My erection slowly started to disappear. I didn't want to look at myself getting fucked. That was just going to remind me of one thing. The thing I had been trying to suppress all summer long.

"Let's do it!" I overeagerly said. I wanted to please him, just like yesterday. I didn't want to cause any friction. I was just going to act like I was into it. But deep down, my anxiety started to increase, and my chest started to compress.

Axel stood up and went for the Sony camcorder that rested on his desk. He picked it up and took his shorts and underwear off whilst he tried to look for the video on the side screen of the camera. He started to touch himself whilst he walked towards me. I sighed. I didn't want to re-live this moment once again. The worst part of it all was that I was going to have to fake it. I was going to have to put on a façade and performance once again. He came to the bed and lay down next to me.

He slowly stroked his penis up and down. "Ready?"

"Yes."

"Well take your shorts off then."

I took my tight athletic shorts off, and then slowly removed my pair of boxers. My penis was soft. I wasn't hard. This wasn't turning me on. This was just pure masochism.

"Okay baby let's watch it… I'm so excited…! Come on, get near me." He grabbed the camcorder with his left hand, and with his right hand he started to masturbate.

The sex tape started to play. I could see my face on the video. I looked scared and vulnerable. I looked upset. The way Axel was holding my head whilst he fucked my mouth looked forceful and aggressive. I was getting exploited. Axel kept jerking his cock harder and harder. I touched myself and attempted to stroke my penis but was unable to get an erection.

"Ugh baby, the way you sucked my dick was so hot!" he started to audibly moan.

I looked at the side screen of the camera and felt like I already wanted to drive to a bridge to jump right off from it. I didn't like to see myself getting mouth fucked. I didn't like to see the derogative and sinful way Axel treated my body on video. But I tried to convince myself that this was Axel's way of showing me his love and affection.

The sex tape glitched and blinked. The video quality was shit. But good enough to tell that Axel was fucking Tony doggy-style. Axel looked at the side-screen with fervent thrill and passion. It was the best porn he had ever watched. It was better than any porn magazine he had ever owned. But this was pure torture and torment for me. This was prosecution. Axel was too focused on himself and the violent action in the video that he didn't even realize that I was barely touching myself whilst watching it. His grunting got louder and louder. His arms started to shake, and his legs started to tremble.

"Baby, I fucked you so good last night!" he moaned, "You took my dick so well!" He jerked his cock in such a hostile and belligerent manner.

I remained mute.

He was starting to reach climax; he closed his eyes and clenched his jaw. He dropped the camera on the bed. He grabbed my arm and grasped it strenuously with his nails. He came on his tight red tee at the same time he ejaculated inside of my ass in the sex tape. Semen dripped all over the cartoon sunshine in the middle of his T-shirt. My penis lay soft between my legs. I was extremely uncomfortable and strained. My brain was spiralling, and I felt like I was on the verge of having a panic attack. The only person I could see penetrating me in the sex tape whilst I watched it was Father Orlando.

Axel brutishly lurched his head onto his pillow and caught his breath. After a few moments, he opened his eyes and gave me a long-prolonged kiss on the lips.

"I love you," he gingerly said.

I remained wordless.

"You know that right…?"

"You are lying," I snapped back.

He leaned backwards and took his arm off around me. "What do you mean?"

"No one has ever said that before," I pulled my boxers up, followed by my shorts.

Axel's tee was still plastered with semen. And his penis and testicles were still out.

"Well, I *do* love you," he leaned towards me. He put his hand on my shoulder. But I quickly dashed it off my body.

I felt gross and disgusted. I didn't know what to say.

"What's wrong?" he asked. I could tell he was worried. My mood had suddenly changed abruptly, and it took him off guard.

"You are lying," my throat started to knot, and tears started to pour down my eyes. "That's what all men do. They just lie," I put my hands on my face and started to uncontrollably sob. I felt stripped and exposed. The emotions I had been holding onto for so long had finally gone loose. Axel tried to hug me, but I pushed him off. "All men want to do is to manipulate you," I screamed. Snot gushed from the nostrils of my nose to the cupid's bow of my lips. "They don't believe in love. They just believe in abuse and exploitation. They just like to use me as their victim. Because they know I'm weak and vulnerable!" I shrieked at the top of my lungs. "And you – that's all you are – you are just like all of them!"

"Why would you ever think that about me? —"

"Why the fuck would you ask me to be your boyfriend after one day of meeting me?" I barked back.

"Because I love you Tony – I want to be with *you* Tony," he held my shoulders with both of his arms tightly.

"You want to hurt me!" I shouted at his face, "You want to abuse me!"

"Where the fuck are you getting this from Tony?"

"I never wanted to do that sex tape!"

"Then why did you never tell me?"

"You forced me to do it!"

"No, I didn't!"

"YES, YOU DID!"

"TONY, WHAT THE FUCK? YOU NEVER SAID ANYTHING!" Axel's face went bright red. His eyes started to well up. I had never seen him lose control like that.

"I'm sorry," I put my hands on my face and vociferously wept, "I'm sorry I never said anything—"

Axel looked at me. Emotionless. He didn't know what to do or what to say.

My lungs began to hyperventilate. I looked like a complete utter mess. "I should have said something."

"Yes, you should've," Axel clapped back. He was furious and angry. "If you had communicated to me that you didn't want to do it, I would have never ever forced you to do it."

I tried to recompose myself, but I was unable to do so. "I just didn't want to disappoint you."

"You would have never disappointed me. I would have respected your decision regardless," he started to cry, "now you've made me feel like I've forced you to do everything we've done together."

"No, no, I swear I've wanted to do everything else."

"How am I going to be sure that you are not lying?"

"Axel. I promise."

Axel wiped away his tears. He felt attacked. He felt like a criminal who hadn't committed any type of crime. "Tony, I don't know what to say. You've ruined this night for both of us—"

"Axel. WHAT THE FUCK? YOU CAN'T SAY THAT!" I slapped him on the face. "I'm sorry—I'm sorry," I quickly apologised. I was feeling volatile and out of control.

"YOU ARE BASICALLY SAYING THAT I'VE ABUSED YOU!" he struck back, "And don't you EVER, EVER, hit me again!"

I started to cry harder and buried my face on the pillow. My back heavily shook. My whole body was trembling. I had ruined this for both of us. This was going to be the end of it. I had hurt Axel and I didn't know how to take it back.

After a short while, Axel put his hand on my pandering shoulder and shifted me around. He held me and hugged me tightly. He gave me a kiss on the forehead. *'Thank God.'*

"Look, I'm sorry," he looked down at his legs. He was unable to see me in the eyes, "You have every right to feel angry and uncomfortable... I just didn't know that you didn't want to do it."

"I'm sorry," I grabbed his left hand tightly.

"No, I *am* sorry. I'm going to delete the video—" He jumped out of the bed.

"No, don't do it," I bawled.

"Yes. I will. You didn't feel comfortable."

"Keep it. Please... I never want to forget us."

"Okay... It will only be for *us* then."

"You promise...?"

"I promise."

I snugged and wrapped myself around Axel's chest. The semen on his tee had dried up. His heart was beating fast, I could tell that he didn't want to have an argument with me. I could tell that he was scared to lose me. And I was scared too. But there was something else lurking on the surface. It wasn't the matter of the sex tape anymore. Something else had been unleashed. The memory I had been trying to suppress all my life since I was fifteen re-emerged. I had never told anyone about it ever in my life. I had to tell someone. Or else I was going to explode. The reason Axel and I had a fight wasn't because I was upset about the sex tape, it was because it reminded me of when Father Orlando raped me.

"Axel... I'm really sorry," I looked up at him shamefully.

"Don't worry about it," he squished my shoulder tightly.

"I swear it wasn't your fault—"

"I said it's fine." He kept staring at the distance.

"Are you still upset...?"

"No... I'm just a little bit drained."

We both remained silent. We had never had a fight before. I didn't like the tension that I felt in the air after the argument. It was going to take us some time to get back to normal. But before that, I had to address the big elephant in the room. It was time to let out the thing that had been haunting me all throughout my teenagehood to my early adult years. The thing that had made my heart rot and my arteries clot.

"Can I tell you something?" I asked.

"Yeah."

I sighed, "This is something I've never told anyone ever before."

"Okay..." He didn't seem that intrigued. But I had to tell him.

"There's just something that has been eating me up all my life," I could start to feel a lump growing in my throat, "it's the reason why I sometimes have these abrupt and sudden mood swings." He could tell that I was starting to break down once again. He began to look at me more seriously. "I didn't mean to scream at you or hit you... I really *am* sorry," I wiped off my tears, "but sometimes, there is this person that still haunts me to this very day." I breathed in and out. "A person that did something really bad to me." My heart palpitated off-beat. "And he comes to me when I least expect it and I don't know what to do with it," I started to clench the sheets of the bed with my hands tightly, "that's why I have these breakdowns and I take it out on the people I love the most." I could see Father Orlando's face gleaming upon me when I closed my eyes. "This person took my childhood and happiness away." I could hardly breathe now.

"Tony, what are you talking about?" Axel reached for my face gently. He was bewildered and confused.

"Axel. Someone raped me when I was fifteen."

Axel stayed speechless; he didn't know what to say.

"And ever since, I've felt like I haven't been able to live," I loudly suspired, "I feel like the only way I could be able to live again would be by killing him," I looked up at Axel, "to erase him from existence."

"Who is this person?"

I gulped. I couldn't say it. "Someone."

"WHO?" Axel's eyebrows furrowed, I could tell that his blood was starting to boil and seethe.

"My high school teacher."

Axel's jaw dropped.

Father Orlando was my Religious studies high school teacher in The Holy Cross of San Lorenzo Catholic Boys School. I hated school with all my might. And I hated Catholicism. All the boys in school made fun of me and hated me. I hated to wear the uniform. It was tight and uncomfortable. And it made me look just like the others. Just like Sunday school, I never was able to fit in. I was the black sheep inside the institution even though we all dressed the same. I was Satan's child and disciple. Religious studies class was my least favourite subject in school. I hated Father Orlando. He was fat and he was ugly. And his breath stank like a rotten swamp. He loathed me too. I was wicked and mischievous and always talked throughout his lessons. I never paid attention to his presentations, and I always audibly laughed during them. I wasn't scared of expressing my hate towards him. He used to expel me out of his classroom when I would talk over him. And he used to send me to the principal's office whenever I would speak back at him. I was fifteen and rude. I would have been any teacher's worst nightmare.

I still remember the day it all happened. It was the fourth of May 1991. The gloomiest Thursday of my life. I used to have Religious studies class every Thursday in the morning at 10AM. This specific day was the day I had to turn in my end of school year printed Christianity report. It was a report where you had to study one religion and write about it extensively. It was the final project of that class. I was fifteen and careless. I had already been traumatised by my mother, the cupboard on the basement of my house, and the crosses that hung on the walls of my living room and staircase. I had no interest in doing this project or turning it in.

At the end of the class, Father Orlando asked everyone to turn in their printed final report at his desk. Every boy in my class walked toward his desk and dropped their final assessment and walked out of the classroom. I was the only one left. I walked up towards him wary and scared.

"Where is your final report, Antonio?" he authoritatively asked me.

"I forgot it in my house…"

"Nonsense!" he snapped back.

"I really did."

"Well, you knew that today was the deadline, and it is the only day I will receive it."

"I'm sorry…" I despairingly whispered. The room was dark, and the shutters were closed. I was facing a tyrannical villain.

"I'm going to have to put you in detention—"

"No, please—"

"Those are the rules of the school, I'm afraid."

"Sorry, I *really* forgot it. I'll bring it to you tomorrow," I pleaded with both of my juvenile shaking hands.

"Meet me today at my office at 5PM after school. I am going to put you to work—"

"No—" I shrieked.

"And if you don't come, I will fail you and tell the principal and your parents." Father Orlando grabbed the papers on his desk, his notebook and his pen. "I'll see you then," he sarcastically smiled and walked out of the room.

I was left there in the classroom all by myself dumbfounded and frightened.

Oh no. That was not good. If I failed, Mother was going to lock me inside the cupboard in the basement again. Mother was going to disown me. I couldn't fail. *'Both of my parents were paying a fortune for me to be here. I couldn't do this to them.'*

I walked out of the classroom. The bell rang.

It was 5PM. All the other boys were walking around the hallways of the school, getting ready to leave. It was the end of the school day. Teachers were going out to the parking lot to their cars. Parents were picking up their children. The school slowly started to look more like an abandoned ghost town as time passed by, but I had to stay. I had to go all the way to Father Orlando's office at the end of the hallway of the sixth floor.

I walked up the stairs to the sixth floor. I was tired and hungry. The corridor was silent and empty. There was no one there except Father Orlando all the way in his office, at the other end of the hallway. The fluorescent lights above me were dim and faint and flickered sinisterly. I arrived at his office. Room 623. I knocked. No one answered. I knocked again. I heard someone standing up from a chair in the interior of the room. Father Orlando answered the door.

"Hello, Mister," he said contemptuously.

"Hello," I looked down at the floor and caught a glimpse of his feet. He had no shoes on.

"Come on in."

I walked inside the room. The room was small and stuffy. It was dark. The blinds were down. And there was no air flow. He closed the door behind me.

"Sit down," he gestured towards the chair in front of his desk.

I sat down. He closed the door and slowly locked it. *'Why was he locking the door?'*

He sat down in front of me. There was a cross hanging on the wall behind him. That was a bad sign. Every time I had seen a cross in my life, it was a sign that something really bad was going to happen. But I tried to ignore it. I breathed in and out, and prepared myself for what he was about to say. My armpits started to sweat, permeating my white cotton shirt.

"Well, Mister… I think you know why you are here."

I looked confused. I was frightened. Something was off. I was unable to speak.

"Don't look at me like that."

"Like what?" I whispered; my voice was quivering.

"You know exactly what you did." He brusquely put his hands on the table.

"Sorry. I told you I could give it to you tomorrow—"

"Can I ask you something Tony?" he charily asked.

"Yeah…"

"Have you ever sinned?"

"No," I swallowed my saliva.

"Don't lie to me Tony," he looked at me directly in the eyes. He was staring me down.

"I didn't."

"Now, tell me, are you a homosexual, Antonio?" he recited my legitimate full name. He looked at me with utter bafflement and disgust.

"No…"

"You are lying to me again," he creepily smiled, "I can see how you look at the boys around you."

"What are you talking about?" I angrily shouted. *'Why was he asking me these questions?', 'I thought this was supposed to be a detention, not an interrogation!'*

"Have you ever sucked dick?" He vulgarly licked his upper lip.

I loudly gulped. I started to get scared. This wasn't going to end pretty. I could tell he wanted to hurt me. I could tell he wanted to do something ungodly to me. "No," I answered, looking down at my feet. My vision started to blur. I was incapable of seeing his face.

He stood up and walked up towards me. *'What was he doing?'*

He slowly unbuckled his belt. "Have you ever had the curiosity to see what it would feel like to suck a dick?"

"No…" I kept looking down at my feet. I was flabbergasted and stupefied. *'This can't be real.'*

"You are still lying," he chuckled. He dashed his pants down. "Look at me."

I turned around and saw an erection protruding from his tight underwear.

"Do you want to fail, Tony?" He tossed his trousers on the floor.

"No…" I quietly mumbled.

He snatched my chin towards his groin. "I'll give you an A+ if you suck my dick."

"No, please, I don't want to!" I dashed his hand away from me.

"Unless you want to fail… You know your mother isn't going to be happy."

I looked up at him. He looked down on me. His fat chin pressed against his corpulent chest. "I don't want to do this," I whimpered.

"I'll tell the principal you did something really bad… and I will get you expelled."

I looked down at the floor. I started to disassociate. I had never felt a feeling like that before. He grabbed my chin again and pulled it towards him.

"Come on, be a good boy," he winked at me, "take my underwear off and suck it!"

I kept staring down at the floor. I froze to death. I didn't know what to do. He got frustrated and loudly groaned. He took his underwear off and stuffed his erect penis inside my mouth. I started to cry. He started to violently thrust his penis inside of my face.

"Ugh, boy, just like that!" he moaned. He grabbed the back of my head tightly and yanked my hair backwards.

I gagged and felt like I was going to vomit. I quickly took the penis out of my mouth.

"Suck it again, you faggot!" he screamed at me like his servant. I had suddenly become his clandestine underage sex slave. He drilled his penis inside my mouth again. He was mouth fucking me. The sound of his testicles thumping on my chin whilst he hammered my mouth was excruciatingly loud. Tears streamed down my face. I was getting abused. This was the first penis I had ever sucked in my life. And it tasted like rotten wretched fish.

He took his penis out of my mouth. "Get on your knees, I'm going to fuck you!"

"What?" I answered back, frightened for my life.

"Get on that desk – now – you whore!" he aggressively shouted at my face, spitting on me with his corrupt and wicked saliva.

"FATHER-PLEASE-STOP!" I squealed.

He grabbed me from the neck and pushed me towards the wall. "YOU DO AS I SAY!"

I started to weep and sob. He put both of his hands on my neck and started to aggressively choke me. I was unable to breathe.

"NOW TURN AROUND!" he roared at me like an outlawed tyrant. No one was at school anymore to hear what was happening.

I turned around. He unbuckled my belt and took my pants and underwear down. He stroked his penis back and forth ferally. He put his hand on my mouth and the other one on my waist. I tried to scream but I was unable to. I just remembered that I wanted to close my eyes. I tried to remind myself that this wasn't really happening. This was all just a nightmare. He pierced his penis right through me. I had never had a penis inside my body until that moment. I wasn't familiar to that kind of pain. His penis was coarse and dry inside my rectum. I screeched and howled and tried to move, but he held me captive with his hands and arms. His plump overweight obese body painfully thumped the back of my scrawny fifteen-year-old body. He held my jaw and mouth tightly with his hand, making sure I wasn't making any kind of noise. '*This wasn't the way I wanted to lose my virginity.*' He pounded my innocent untouched ass cheeks roughly. He groaned on my ears with his putrid-coffee stinking breath. He bit my earlobes and growled deafeningly. I became a vegetable; I no longer was there. I stopped moving, as all the hope I had was lost. He was penetrating a dead corpse.

Like a paedophile and necrophiliac, Father Orlando raped me under the cross that hung on his wall. He ejaculated his crimes

137

inside of my rectum. He leaned his forehead on the back of my neck and caught his breath. After a few seconds, he reached for his underwear and pants on the floor and intrinsically put them on. I stayed attached to the wall with my glutes bare naked exposed. I couldn't move. I was petrified and frozen. Medusa had turned me into stone. I could feel the cruelty in this world. The type of cruelty I thought God had already eradicated from this earth. My heart stopped beating. I didn't want to see him. I was scared to see his face. I looked up at the cross above me and sighed. Crosses didn't like me.

"I guess we know who is getting an A+ now," Father Orlando articulated, trying to make me feel a little bit more comfortable after he had raped me.

I turned around and looked at him. He could see the expression on my face. I was destroyed.

"Oh, don't look at me like that," he said, "I know you liked it." He winked at me in a malevolent manner as he fixed his black tie and tightened up his pants.

I remained speechless. I pulled my underwear and trousers up. My anus hurt. I could feel that my anal tissues had been teared apart.

"Tony!" he pulled my arm roughly, "You tell this to anyone, and your life is over!"

I looked down at the floor, trying to avoid eye contact.

"LOOK AT ME!" he screamed.

I looked up at him with fright and terror.

"If anyone finds about this, I am going to kill you," he sinisterly enunciated every syllable and word of that sentence, looking at me directly in the eyes with absolute repugnance and hatred, "and will ruin your life forever!" But he had already ruined it. I wish he had killed me just then. "AND I MEAN IT!"

I was scared for my life and believed that if I ever spoke about it to anyone, he was in fact going to murder me or ruin my life. But no one was ever going to believe me if I ever opened up to someone about it. I was never going to be able to deal with that level of shame and embarrassment.

"Do you understand?" he asked, pulling my arm tighter towards him.

"Yes Father."

He pushed me. "Now get out of my office! I have work to do."

I took my backpack from the floor, adjusted my hair, and tightened my white cotton shirt and walked out.

I walked through the corridor. The sky outside the windows was apocalyptically grey. There was no one else in the building. I was going to have to go home and act like none of this had happened. I was going to have to live my life like I had never been raped. I was going to have to suppress this memory for the rest of my life. I started to well up and as I walked down the stairs of the building, I thought to myself, *'One day, I am going to get stronger, and I'm going to kill him.'*

X

Carnage

Leviticus 24:19-21

"Anyone who injures their neighbour
is to be injured in the same manner:
fracture for fracture, eye for eye, tooth for tooth.
The one who has inflicted the injury must suffer the same
injury. Whoever kills an animal must make restitution,
but whoever kills a human being is to be put to death."

The story I had hidden all my life had finally sprung loose. The shadow that used to haunt me in my sleep every night had finally been exposed to the light. I had finally spoken about the man who had taken my virginity away at fifteen. My hands were shaking. My legs were trembling. My voice was quivering. But it felt good. It felt good to speak about it. My neck and cheeks were drenched by the wetness of my tears. Blood rushed rapidly throughout my veins and arteries. I felt triggered and electrified all at once. An adrenaline rush I had never felt before. The story I thought I was going to have to take with me to the grave had been listened by the man I had ever loved the most.

Axel looked down at the floor. He was picking his nails. His penis and testicles were still out. I had never seen his penis that soft and flimsy before. I could tell everything I had disclosed had affected him in another level. It had already been a very draining evening. We had a big, heated argument moments before. The night was hot, and the room was extremely stuffy. I wiped my tears off and tried to look for reassurance in Axel. He remained mute and silent. His hair covered his face. But I could tell something was wrong. I could feel it across my chest. Axel didn't have to utter a word for me to understand what was going on. But I still asked.

"What's wrong?" I asked him with my weeping snot-stuffed nose voice.

He stayed silent. He repeatedly moved his knee up and down. His mind was no longer with me. It had gone somewhere else.

"Hey, what's up?" I leaned on him, and gently put my hand on his left stubbled cheek.

He looked up at me. His eyes were bloodshot red. His face was purple plump. I had never seen anger and violence expressed on a human face before like that. The way his eyebrows furrowed above his eyes portrayed this fervent rage and frenzy.

"Baby, what's wrong? —" I asked again. I was greatly confused.

"Where does he live?" he savagely interrupted me.

"What do you mean?" I answered back bewildered and perplexed. I didn't know what was going on anymore.

"Do you know where he lives?"

"No... I don't know—" I looked up at him. I could see the primitive violence in the pupils of his eyes.

"Well, you better tell me now!" He quickly stood up and reached for his boxers on the floor. He started to put them on abruptly.

"What are you doing?" I grasped on his arm, stopping him. He pushed me back and put his baggy denim shorts on. "Axel, STOP! What are you doing?"

"I'm going to fuck him up – I swear – I'm going to fuck him up!"

"Axel, Stop!" I pushed him back to the bed and took hold of his arms.

"LET ME GO!" he shouted at my face.

"Axel! You can't react like that!" I wrestled with his strong beefy arms.

"I said *LET ME GO!*" he screamed at me once again and scratched my arms. His voice cracked at the end of his scream. I had never seen him react that way ever. It was masculine, impulsive and scary. I let go of him.

Axel started wailing. I had never seen a man cry with such lament. It was painful and enduring to watch. My body was above his. '*Shouldn't I be the one who should be reacting like this?*' Like a little child that had lost his red car toy, Axel loudly wept and sobbed. I didn't know what to do. I was motionless. The man that had dominated me on bed every night for the past two weeks of my life had suddenly been defeated and weakened by an unknown force. I placed my face on his chest, like I always used to do, and held both of his pectorals tightly with each hand. His T-shirt was drenched in sweat and dried-up cum. He was hyperventilating, and tears kept brutally rushing down his face. He was unable to stop crying. I had opened a door he probably never wanted to open ever again.

"I WANT TO LEAVE THIS PLACE!" he cried out, "I WANT TO LEAVE THIS COUNTRY!" Axel kept weeping like a child. But this wasn't a tantrum. This was something real. And painful.

"Axel, what are you on about?"

"Tony – please – you have t-to lea-leave with me," he stumbled on his words; his nose was incredibly stuffed.

"Axel, please—"

"Tony, this city, this country, this place has destroyed my life!"

I felt butterflies in my stomach. I felt a rush of blood coming to my brain. The man in front of me had felt the same way I did for the entirety of my life. "Axel! —"

"Tony, my uncle raped me when I was twelve." He put his hands on his face and started to sob again.

I felt a lump in my throat. My heart stopped for a second. I didn't know what to say. I wasn't alone in this. Another person had experienced the same thing I did in this town, in this city, in this country. "I'm sorry…" I got up from his chest and looked at him with a certain quality of dismay.

He wiped his tears off. And loudly sighed. "You are the first person I have ever told."

"Axel, you are the first person I have ever told *too*."

We both looked at each other in disbelief. The feeling and aftertaste you get in your mouth after vomiting is what we both felt. We didn't feel good, but we felt better. We both had finally let it all out. By accident and out of coincidence, we had both confessed our darkest and deepest secrets to each other. I held his hand tightly and smiled at him. I suddenly stopped feeling alone. But I could tell Axel's mind was still spiralling ferociously.

"Thank you for telling me," I delicately murmured.

"Thank you, as well."

Axel stood up and walked towards the window. The moon shone radiantly across the wooden tiles of the room. It was full moon. All of the stars and planets had aligned. It was the best time to plan and scheme something unlawful and criminal.

The clock struck twelve. Midnight had started. It was the twentieth of August 1996. Axel's mood and character had suddenly changed. The atmosphere was fretful and tense. We were both silent, but we could still hear the quick and hurried rhythm of our hearts. We both knew that confessing these stories wasn't enough. There was still something left to do. There was still unfinished business left. The ceiling fan above us spun at the speed of lightning, attempting to air our thoughts out. Axel paced the room back and forth. Something specific was on his mind.

Anxiety radiated all throughout his body.

"What are you thinking?" I asked.

"Nothing."

"Axel, don't lie to me."

"I said nothing."

"Axel – tell me exactly what you are thinking," I answered back firmly.

"It's fucked up…"

"Axel, fuck off!"

"No, no, Tony, I'm not kidding, this is *really* fucked up."

"What could be more fucked up than what we have already told each other?"

He looked back at me. "Tony, I feel scared that I'm capable of doing something." His eyes were no longer watery or bloodshot red. They were jade green stark like emerald stone.

I crawled to the end of the bed in desperation. "Capable of doing what?"

"Capable of killing someone," he said with firm verdict and decision.

I looked at him puzzled and perplexed. "You are not going to kill me, are you?" I said sarcastically.

"I would never kill you. Ever—"

"Axel, come on, its late, let's go to sleep—" I moved towards the headboard of the bed expecting him to come back to bed.

"I was never able to kill my own uncle…" Axel looked out of the window, lost in his own little world and thoughts.

"Axel, what are you on about?" I got out of the bed and started to walk towards him near the window.

"God killed him," Axel remarked, "God did it without asking

me. And ever since then, I have hated God."

I took his hands and tried to reassure him. "Axel—"

"He died of lung cancer at the age of fifty-nine," Axel pushed my hands away and tucked his hair behind his ears, "but I wanted to kill him myself. I wanted to make him pay for what he did to me."

Blood rushed rapidly into my cheeks. I had had that same exact feeling before. The feeling of wanting to kill the person that had ruined and tainted your life forever. The feeling I had been trying to supress all my life since Father Orlando raped me. "I understand that feeling. Axel."

Axel looked at me directly in the eyes. "I never got to do it. I was too scared."

"I wish I could do it too, but I don't want to rot in jail or hell... you know?" I nervously laughed.

"I have been regretting it all my life," Axel took hold of my cheek tightly, "cancer beat me to it. I was never able to seek revenge."

"I'm sorry, Axel." I didn't know what else to say. My hands started to shake. The feeling Axel was experiencing moments before had started to manifest within me. I could feel the violence and anger starting to rush inside of me. The primitive and bestial version of myself had been uncontrollably unleashed.

"But you can," Axel firmly said.

"What do you mean?"

"You still have the opportunity to kill Father Orlando," Axel put both of his hands behind my neck.

I stayed silent. What would have sounded like nonsense and utter madness to me a few minutes ago began to sound plausible and reasonable. My heart started to beat faster and faster. And not out of nervousness, but of excitement. I looked up at him mystified and bemused.

"I can help you," he whispered.

"How?" I answered. The Devil had finally possessed me. I no longer felt remorse or guilt. The need of wanting to kill Father Orlando started to increase more and more as time passed by. I no longer cared about the consequences I could face. I could only think about the feeling of seeing his blood splatter on my body, knowing that I was the one who took his life away, the same way he took mine a few years ago. Axel could see it in my eyes. I was ready to commit murder.

"This is why I love you. You are as crazy and mad as me." He intensely kissed me on the lips.

I took hold of him and separated him from my face. "Are you serious?" I asked in disbelief.

"How do you want to kill him? With a gun or a knife?" he villainously chuckled.

Motionless, I could not get a word out of my mouth. This was no longer a joke. We were both scheming and planning a legitimate murder now. "I d-don't k-know…"

"Depends how bloody you want it."

"But how are we going to do it? —What if we get caught? —"

"Do you know where he lives…?"

I gulped. There was no going back. Something had changed within me. If I didn't take this opportunity now, I was going to regret it for the rest of my life. This was going to allow me to change my life completely. Axel and I were going to kill Father Orlando. I no longer was alone in this. "I think he lives in McArdle Road, two blocks away from my high school. My school bus used to pass his house every morning. His house is small. It has a grey façade and a blue rooftop. He lives alone, but I'm not sure if he still lives there."

"Do you want to risk it?" Axel subtly smirked. He pushed his forehead against mine. Rays of moonlight beamed right through the space between both of our faces.

I swallowed my saliva. I was unable to speak again. I no longer felt nervous or terrorized. I could feel a burst of exhilaration and happiness. The type of flush you get after smoking a joint. I could feel a big smile starting to grow on my face. This was not funny. This was not a joke. Axel and I were serious about this. I couldn't stop fantasizing about a world where Father Orlando didn't exist. But even better, I couldn't stop romanticizing about a world where the victim finally gets to avenge his abuser and wipes him off the face of this earth.

"I said, do you want to risk it?" Axel muttered, placing one hand on my lower back and the other one on my ass.

"Yes," I replied with a big smile on my face. Axel kissed me on the lips. The thrill and excitement of this Machiavellian arrangement triggered a long passionate wet tongue make out. My brain was filled with questions. But I had already stopped thinking. I had finally surrendered to Satan. "What are we going to do after, though?"

"What do you mean?" Axel laughed.

"Yeah... what are we going to do? — We can't just stay here..."

Axel marched towards his nightstand swiftly. He grabbed his car keys and threw them to me.

I caught the keys with one hand. "What does this mean?" I was spellbound.

Axel paced back to me swiftly. "We will go to Mexico."

"Are you mad?"

"Do *you* want to stay here?"

"No..."

"Exactly... We'll drive to Mexico, and no one will ever see us or hear about us ever again," Axel wrapped himself around my chest and arms.

"But—"

"No, buts," Axel put his index finger on my lips, "shhh… It will all be alright."

"But my parents, my family—"

"Let's be honest… do you like them?"

"No…"

"Exactly."

I knew I couldn't deny this opportunity either. Satan sent me an opportunity to escape from this hellish heaven. The hypocritical infernal heaven that was Corpus Christi, Texas. I couldn't say no. Nothing made sense. Everything felt like a fever dream. I was still waiting to wake up from this ludicrous dream. I had always wanted to escape from my family. I had always wanted to escape from this place, from this country.

"Are you going to love me forever?" I anxiously asked.

Axel kissed me once again, holding my lower back. "I will love you, forever and ever."

I glanced down at the floor and pondered for a second. "Okay… Yes…" I looked up at him directly in the eyes. "I want to flee to Mexico with you… And only you."

"When should we do it, then? —"

"Tonight!" I took the back of his head with my hands tightly. "I want to kill him tonight… And I want to escape to Mexico tonight…"

"Tonight?" Axel asked, deeply entranced.

"Yes. Tonight… I want to do it before I regret it."

"You are absolutely mad," Axel smiled at me. He kissed me once again. "Let's do it!"

I took hold of his hand tightly. "I wouldn't want to do it with anyone else."

"I love you," Axel murmured. Axel put my hand on his chest. I could feel his heartbeat. "I have never felt this excited in my life ever before."

I took Axel's hand and placed it on my beating heart. "Me neither."

We both looked at each other. We were both deeply in love. We were both going to commit crime. And we were both going to escape to Mexico from this abominable shithole.

It was 1:30AM. The clock kept ticking. Time was upon us. Axel was shoving clothes into his backpack rapidly. He threw his wallet at me.

"Keep that. I have a stash of money there."

I put his wallet on the pocket of my shorts.

"We will drive to yours to get your stuff before we head to his house." He kept pushing clothes and shoes inside his bag. He was stressed and frustrated.

"Let me help you," I took the bag out of his hands, "do you have your passport?"

"Shit, you're right!!!" He padded the back of his shorts and started to go through the papers of his desk brusquely and hurriedly, trying to find it. He then went to his chest of drawers and opened a drawer. He threw clothes and drapes to the floor. "Found it!"

"Okay… We must fucking go now!" I hollered.

"Okay, okay, you have my wallet, right?"

"Yes."

Axel put his backpack around his shoulders and put his shoes on. I already had mine on. "Let's go!" Axel fervently shouted.

We were extremely unprepared. I didn't have a good feeling about this. My brain became an endless spiral. "Wait—but how are we going to kill him?"

"Up to you..." Axel scratched the back of his head.

"I don't know..." I shrieked.

We both looked at each other. We hadn't figured out the most important thing yet.

"My father has a charged revolver hidden in one of the drawers of the kitchen," Axel fiendishly suggested.

"Okay..." *Fuck... I've never used a gun before...'* I thought to myself.

"You know how to shoot?"

"No..."

"For, fuck's sake—"

I checked the clock on his wall. "We have to go now."

"Ugh... Fuck it... It's easy. I'll show you in the car."

"Okay! Let's go...! Hurry the fuck up!"

Axel checked he had everything on him. He quickly scouted the room.

"AXEL!"

"Okay—Let's go!" Axel walked towards the door of his room and opened it. "Be quiet!" He tiptoed out of his room. I followed him from behind.

I waited inside of Axel's cherry-red Jetta in the driveway outside of his house. Axel had gone to the kitchen to fetch the gun. I could hardly breathe. I could hardly move my body. I had never felt so much terror and excitement at the same time in my life ever before.

Axel opened the door of the car and got in.

"Got it?" I nervously asked.

"Yes," he handed me the revolver. The gun was heavy. "Hide it!"

I put it below the passenger seat.

"Drive to my house," I commanded.

Axel turned the engine on and zoomed out of his driveway.

Axel waited inside his cherry-red Jetta a block away from my house. Both of my parents' cars were in the driveway. I opened the door of my house quietly. My parents' bedroom was shut. The living room was dark and opaque. The crosses that plagued the wall of my house looked at me directly in the eyes, disapproving of the crimes I was about to commit. Condemning me for the fact that I was going to kill Father Orlando and I was going to abandon my family forever. I noiselessly sprinted up the staircase all the way to my bedroom on the third floor.

I quickly undressed myself. I put a pair of new underwear. I threw on a pair of Realtree Camo pants and a black cotton ribbed tank top. I grabbed the cash I had from my nightstand and stuffed it inside the pockets of my trousers. I grabbed the backpack that was lying beneath my desk and started to stuff it with all the dirty clothes that were already on the floor. I didn't have time. I crammed a pair of white Nikes, clean underwear and socks. A bomb had just gone off inside my room. The clock kept ticking and my heart kept racing. I got out of my room and started to walk downstairs. *'My passport!'* Oh shit. My passport. *'Where the fuck is it?'* I ran back to my room and started to go through every drawer and cubby-hole. I dashed clothes and objects to the floor. Trying not to be too loud. *'There it is!'* It was all the way in the back of the last drawer of my desk. I took it and jammed it inside my backpack.

I walked downstairs. I opened the front door. I took a deep breath in and out. I looked back at my parents' bedroom door and at the living room that had all our conjoined family pictures. I was going to leave this forever. After this day, everything was going to change. Nothing was ever going to be the same. I felt a painful sensation in my stomach and chest, but deep down I knew that this house had never done me any good. I was excited to know that I would never see Mother's face ever again. I was probably doing her a favour. I looked at the crosses that hung on the walls once again. I was going to finally kill the religion I had been indoctrinated with ever since I was a child. I was going to rotate those crosses upside down. I was going to become a fallen angel. I was going to deceive God. I was going to betray Jesus. But I was going to seek justice and revenge. I was going to seek my own type of happiness and rejuvenation. I took one more deep breath in and out and walked out of the door. I closed it gently. I locked the door and put the keys inside my pocket.

I got inside the cherry-red Jetta and put my backpack beneath my feet. Axel was fidgeting and playing with the revolver whilst he waited for me.

"Are you ready?" he asked.

"I'm ready," I audibly sighed. I could feel my heart pounding inside my head.

He handed me the revolver back. I looked at it closely. I gently held the trigger with my index finger. *'I'm ready to kill!'* I placed it beneath my seat.

Axel turned the ignition switch with his car key.

The engine of the car turned on.

"Let's go...!" he firmly said with a slight smirk across his face.

Axel jetted out of the avenue at warp speed.

XI

Butchery

Genesis 9:5-6

"And for your lifeblood I will surely demand an accounting.
I will demand an accounting from every animal.
And from each human being, too, I will demand
an accounting for the life of another human being.
'Whoever sheds human blood,
by humans shall their blood be shed;
for in the image of God
has God made mankind.'"

The day I had been waiting for all my life had finally arrived. Deep down, in my subconscious I had always wanted to kill Father Orlando since the day he raped me inside of his office all the way in the back of the sixth floor of my high school. But until this night, I was never able to make sense of those volatile and violent primitive feelings I had in the past. Ever since the fourth of May 1991, I had always wanted to seek revenge. I had always wanted to make him pay the price for what he did to me. But I was never able to put those feelings into words. It was something I felt across my chest. A feeling that would make my jaw clench and my teeth squeeze into one another. Because no one will ever understand what it is to get raped, until you get ruthlessly raped. Father Orlando killed me that evening. He took my body away. He turned me into a walking corpse. A bag of skin and bones. He took my purity away. He took my innocence away. He took my virginity away. He took everything from me. But now, it was time to take everything away from him. His own motherfucking life.

153

I had always wondered what it would feel like to kill someone. As a child, I always had intrusive thoughts of snatching the kitchen knife out of Mother's hands and stabbing her across the chest. I had always been curious about the sensation of causing harm to another person. I had thoughts of spilling hot oil on Mother's face. *'Would my consciousness be able to live after doing such a thing?'* Intrusive thoughts had plagued me my entire life. I couldn't walk on a sidewalk without getting intrusive thoughts of pushing someone into the road. I heavily feared those thoughts. *'Why did I have these types of thoughts?', 'And why couldn't I get rid of them?'*

I held the revolver with both of my hands tightly. Axel was behind the wheel. We were going about 85km per hour, going past the speed limit. He was silent. And I was too. I could tell that he was overwrought and nervous. But this was the moment he had been waiting for all his life too. He never got the chance to kill his own abuser, but he was going to watch me kill mine. I looked down at the gun. I had never held one of these ever before. It was heavy. In a matter of minutes, I was going to change my life forever by shooting someone in the head. I was going to take someone's life away. I was going to commit murder. I was going to commit crime. I was going to commit manslaughter. And in a few hours, I was going to become an official 'wanted' criminal. I was going to become the villain. I was going to become the bad guy. I was going to become the criminal that broke into someone's house in the middle of the night and cold-bloodedly shot them dead with a revolver. But no one was ever going to find out about Father Orlando's crimes. No one was ever going to find out what he did to me. How he grabbed my head against his cock and mouth fucked me against my will. How he choked me and pushed me against the wall of his office and forcefully raped me. Father Orlando was going to become the victim, and I was going to become the criminal.

God had cursed me ever since I was born. He cursed me with my family and my mother. He cursed me with my life. He cursed me with this town. He cursed me with Father Orlando. God didn't like me. God had tried to kill me throughout my life in so many ways. But he always miserably failed.

Rape should never be forgiven in God's realm. But God easily forgave Father Orlando. God acted like he had never seen it happen. God was a hypocrite man. God was corrupt. God was a glutinous old man that liked to be worshipped by his dumbfounded weakened peasants. God lived in heaven, in a gated community, like a feudal king, viciously feasting from our pain and suffering. He expelled Satan from heaven, because he knew Satan was more powerful than him. He knew Satan was smarter than him.

I had always had a deeper connection with Satan than with God ever since I was a child. Satan had always been long misunderstood. Satan had been defamed by God. But the real villain was God. He was the bearded man that allowed these crimes to happen. He was the quenchless fat man who pushed little cherubs' mouths onto his thorned throbbing cock, cruelly mouth fucking them whilst he sat on his throne drinking wine. God was a paedophile. He was the man that enjoyed watching priests and fathers abuse little children in the shadows. God was a rapist. He was the man that let Father Orlando rape me. He was the man that masturbated to both of my rape scenes. And today, I was going to finally revolt against him and his crimes. I was going to end the debauchery and corruption within his kingdom. Today was to become my coronation day in the flamed gates of hell. Today was to become the day, Satan and I would become one.

Axel was nervously clenching the stirring wheel with both of his hands. "How are you feeling?"

"I'm nervous." The gun shook in my hand. I was jittering.

"Don't worry. You just have to aim for the head or the chest... And once it's done. It's done."

"Like this? —" I raised the gun and aimed it towards the windshield.

"Be careful!" he shouted, "Don't shoot now!"

"Don't worry, I didn't have my finger in the trigger—"

"Tony, be careful, this is delicate… It's already charged."

"How are we going to do this then?" I looked up at him. We were twenty minutes away from McArdle Road. The freeway was pitch-black. The car hissed on the road. The clock kept ticking.

"Do you want me to wait for you outside while you do it?"

"What? NO! I need someone there with me!" I snapped back.

"Tony! I *have* to be in the car, so we can get the fuck outta there as fast as we can after you do it! —"

"But AXEL! I need you there. What if he attacks me? We need two people there."

"Fine."

"What?"

"But after we do it, we have to sprint back to the car as fast as we can. And fuck our way out to Mexico." Axel gripped the stirring wheel tightly. The stakes were high. The tension in the air was overpowering.

"Do you know how to go to Mexico, though?"

"Yes! You just take the 77 directly. I think it's just a four-hour drive."

"Do we have enough gas?"

Axel stood silent for a second. "Yes. But we'll have to stop somewhere near the border." Axel looked back at me and held my hand tightly. "Don't worry, I've got enough cash."

"I'm nervous, Axel," I responded. My heart had stopped beating a long time ago.

"There is nothing you need to be nervous about," Axel reassured me, "after you kill him, we will run to the car to drive to Mexico immediately… The police will only find out about the murder after a few days. But by then, we will already be in Mexico… Missing… Erased from existence… No one will ever find us."

"Okay," I exhaled. I had my right hand on the gun and the other one on Axel's warm clammy palm. "We got this," I said, trying to reassure myself.

Axel nodded and kept driving. We were getting close.

It was 3AM. The hour of the Devil. Axel parked on McArdle Road. In front of the grey-façade house and blue-hued rooftop. Father Orlando's house. It was number fifty-seven. His grey Volkswagen beetle was parked on his driveway. He still lived there. The street was quiet, reminiscent to an apocalyptical ghost town. The streetlamps were dim and dull. Owls sinisterly hooted. Everyone was asleep. Even the dogs.

Axel turned the engine off and loudly sighed, "We are here."

I could feel the blood pumping from my heart to the jugular vein of my neck. I looked down at the gun. My hands were quivering. I vociferously sighed.

"Are you ready?" Axel asked.

"Yes," I closed my eyes slowly.

"Okay, let's do it—" Axel unbuckled himself and started to open the front seat door.

"WAIT!" I screamed.

"What?" Axel silently closed the door of the car.

"Let's do a prayer first."

Axel sarcastically laughed. "What… To God? He most definitely doesn't connote this—"

"No… to Satan."

"To Satan?" Axel looked up at me deeply perplexed.

"Yes… We'll put this on his hands. He'll guide us through it—"

"Are you a satanist!?"

"No."

"Then why are you doing this?"

"It doesn't matter," I whispered, "God has done both of us dirty either way."

"He has."

"Okay, give me your hand."

Axel gave me his hand.

I grabbed it tightly and closed my eyes. "Satan. On this night, Axel and I are going to seek revenge and finally take control of our own lives. We are finally going to kill the person that took my life away. Please assist us and guide us through this experience. We put our name in your faith. Please help us be successful… Oh Hail, Satan!" I nervously laughed. This felt like a joke.

Axel laughed too.

"In the name of the father, the son, and the holy ghost…" I gave Axel a kiss on the lips. "Amen," I grabbed the back of his neck tightly.

He placed his forehead on mine. "I love you."

"I love you too," I replied.

"We will have to break through a window… We can't wake him up."

"I hope he's there."

"He is… I can already feel his dark and gloomy presence." Axel gave me another kiss on the lips and walked out of the car.

I breathed in and out deeply. I took hold of the gun tightly, fixed my hair and opened the car door.

The night was dark. The air was chilly. The atmosphere was

piercing silent. Axel and I stood outside the house. The gun was hidden inside my pocket. I had never felt this way before. This wasn't a plan or a game anymore. I was standing in front of the house of my abuser preparing myself to commit manslaughter, like a prey ready to strike back at its predator.

Axel walked around the exterior of the house trying to find a discrete and subtle window we could break in from. The windows of the living room were big and tall, and that could wake him up. We didn't know where his bedroom was either.

"Tony!" Axel whispered at me from the distance, "Come!" he gestured at me, "Now!"

I tiptoed my way through the dry and coarse Texan suburban grass.

"Here!" Axel signalled towards a small window in the back of the house which looked like the window of a basement.

"That looks promising…" I could hardly talk or breathe, let alone move.

"Pass me the gun!"

"Why?"

"STOP ASKING QUESTIONS!" He snatched the gun out of my pocket and broke the window of the basement with the pistol's grip.

The window of the basement broke. Glass fell onto the wooden dusty floor below.

"Come on! Let's go!" Axel slowly crammed himself through the window and dropped to the floor of the basement.

I followed him. I jammed myself into the window. I couldn't feel my limbs or joints. This had to be one of the scariest things I had ever done in my life. But I wasn't alone. I was here with the love of my life.

The basement was pitch-black. We could hardly see anything. The light that came outside from the window guided us to a wooden staircase all the way in the back. There were cardboard boxes scattered all across the wooden-panelled floors. It reminded me of my basement. The basement where Mother used to lock me in the cupboard for hours after I had committed a sin. The air was stuffy and humid. The dust pierced right through my nostrils. I loudly coughed.

"SHHH!" Axel murmured, "We'll walk upstairs, and we will look for his bedroom. We must be extremely quiet!"

"Okay." I suddenly lost my hearing ability. It almost felt like I was deep down in the depths of a pool. And every sound that came from the outside of the pool was muffled and muted.

Axel walked up the wooden staircase. It creaked. He waited for me to come up all the way where he was. I reached the top of the staircase.

"Ready?" he whispered.

I nodded.

He opened the door of the basement slowly. I didn't want to do this anymore. The thrill and horror consumed my whole body. All my five senses were cruelly overcharged. Axel handed me the revolver. The clock kept ticking. The time to kill him was getting closer and closer.

The basement door led us into the living room. I slowly closed the door behind me. The living room was bare opaque boring. There were two mint green corduroy sofas facing each other and a small cheap plastic coffee table between them, with a bible and rosary on it. The floor was carpeted and looked dirty. There were white and green stains on the carpet. There were some pictures hung on the wall. Mainly pictures of him. There was one picture of him holding his undergraduate degree certificate in college when he was younger. Another one with his priest attire. The pictures were eerie and sinister. The place was uninviting and inhospitable. The living room looked like the house of a serial killer, the houses they used to show in the documentaries about serial killers on the Investigation Discovery channel. The house smelled like burnt red meat. There were various crosses on the walls. *'Oh no. This wasn't a good sign.'* Crosses were my worst nemesis. Something really bad was going to happen.

Axel and I scouted the first floor of the house. We quietly tiptoed our way through the carpets. The house was completely empty. There wasn't much furniture. It was stark and cold. Impersonalized. The moonlight glimmered brightly through the curtains of the living room into this uncanny interior space. We went inside the kitchen. The kitchen was mouldy and dirty. The smell was putrid and musty. A pile of unwashed dirty dishes lay flat on the sink. Garbage bags were tossed and cluttered all the way in the back of the corner. There was a spoiled milk carton left on the counter. This man had no hygiene. His house reflected his rotten and rancid soul.

There was no bedroom to be found on the first floor of the house. The ceilings were high, and the house looked twice as big for the lack of things that inhabited inside the space. I paced behind Axel. He was leading the way. We walked up the stairs of the house.

"Shhhhhh! Be extra quiet!" he whispered.

I walked even more quietly than before.

We reached the second floor of the house. There were three closed doors. One of those doors had to be his bedroom.

The second floor of the house was darker and more obsolete. It smelled like dirty laundry and human sweat.

"Okay, this is it," Axel said.

"Yes." I grabbed the gun tightly with my right hand and my index finger on the trigger.

"It can be any of these doors," Axel stuttered. He closed his eyes and sighed deeply. "Let's go."

Axel opened the first door. The door in front of the staircase. It was an empty room. There were three empty carboard boxes stacked on top of each other all the way in the back of the room. The curtains of the window were wide open. The moonlight kept shining bright. My heart was racing. The blood inside my veins kept pumping faster and faster, the same feeling you would get before riding a roller coaster. Axel walked out of the room rapidly and walked towards the end of the hallway where the last two doors were. I followed him. I gripped the revolver tightly. It could be any time now. This felt like a movie. This didn't feel real. I was about to become a criminal and a cold-blooded murderer in a matter of seconds.

Axel opened the second door. The door in front of the third door. It was the bathroom. The bathroom was white-tiled all throughout. There was yellow mould growing in between the tiles. There was a pair of dirty old boxers on the floor. The air smelled like humid unwashed towels. There was urine in the toilet bowl. The sink was plastered with decayed toothpaste. The mirror was dirty. There was a picture of Jesus Christ pasted onto the mirror, alongside a prayer. Axel walked out of the bathroom with a hand over his mouth and nose. The stench inside of the washroom was intense and smelled like if a corpse had been left rotting there for more than a year. I walked out with him.

This was it. The last door had to be his bedroom.

"This is his bedroom," Axel muttered, "get the gun ready."

I raised the gun in front of me, gripping it tightly with both of my hands, I was ready to shoot. I was ready to kill. I breathed in and out deeply.

"Ready?" Axel asked.

"Ready."

Axel opened the door of the bedroom quietly. He waited by the door. I came in first, he walked behind me. There he was, after years of not seeing him, Father Orlando's body lay deeply asleep on his bed. There was a cross above his headboard. I started to get even more scared. He was loudly snoring. A big hippopotamus under the covers. His neck was even fatter than before. He looked like a monster, worse than he did before. The room smelled like pigskin and stew. I could feel the anger surging up my spine. I could feel the rage consuming my whole body. I could feel my blood seething. I was ready to take the life of the person who took my life first.

"What are you waiting for?" Axel desperately whispered, "Shoot now!"

"No! I want to be the last person he sees before he dies."

"Tony! DO IT!"

"I want him to know that I was the person that took his fucking life away!" I screamed.

Father Orlando woke up startled and frightened.

"What are you doing here?" he howled, "Who are you?" I could see the fear on his face.

I walked towards him. I clenched the revolver tightly with both of my hands. My index finger on the trigger. I was staring him down.

"Get out of my house!" he screamed. He tried to cover his whole body with his sheets and blankets.

I walked closer to him. "Don't you remember who I am?"

He squinted. He looked deeply within my eyes. He recognised me. "Who are you?" he asked, whilst he hyperventilated.

"Don't lie to me," I quickly snapped back, "I'm Tony."

"I don't know who you are or what this is—"

"Put your hands behind your head."

Father Orlando stayed motionless. His jaw dropped.

"I SAID PUT YOUR HANDS BEHIND YOUR HEAD!" I shouted at the top of my lungs.

Father Orlando quickly placed his hands behind his head. I walked closer and closer to him.

"Tony, DO IT NOW!" Axel yelled from the distance.

I put the gun beside his head, with my index finger on the trigger. "Don't you remember me?"

"NO!!!" he sonorously cried. Tears gushed down his ogre-like face. He was petrified and could hardly breathe. "Please. I didn't do anything… Please!"

"I was the fifteen-year-old boy you raped," I firmly said.

"What?" he looked at me completely muddled and confused. I looked deeply into his pupils. He knew exactly who I was. He never expected me to come back. He never expected me to seek revenge.

I pulled the trigger. I shot him dead. Blood splattered on my face and arms. Pieces of his brain flew into the air. His overweight and corpulent body savagely catapulted onto the mattress. I had killed him. I had just killed someone. I had just committed murder. I stayed silent for a second in disbelief of what I had just done. I felt a mass of pain and horror consume my body completely. I screamed and dropped to the floor. The moment I had been waiting for all my life had finally happened before my eyes. In the snap of a finger, my life had already completely changed. I cried and I howled. I was breathless. The extremities of my body rapidly shook side by side. I had blood on my hands. I was tainted with the blood of the man that had raped me.

"Tony! Let's go!" Axel screeched.

I kept weeping and mourning on the floor. Axel ran towards me and attempted to pick me up. "AXEL!" I screamed.

"WHAT??"

"What are we go-going to-tod-do with the b-b-od-d-dy?" I stumbled on my words. My throat was knotted, and my nose was stuffed.

"What do you mean?"

"We can't just leave it here…" I kept gasping for air.

"Tony that was the plan!!!" Axel's soul had already left his body.

"We have to get rid of it—"

"HOW?" Axel screamed, pulling on his hair. Time was upon us, and the clock kept ticking.

"We need to carry it somewhere and dispose of it." I wiped my tears off. I feared for both of our lives.

"WHEREE?!?"

"In the 'Rio del Rosario'!"

"Tony, I'm going to fuck you up! —This was never the plan! —We were just going to leave him here and go!"

"Axel. We must do it!"

"FUCK!!!" Axel howled. He caught his breath and after a few moments he agreed. "Okay… We gotta get this body to the ground floor somehow then—"

"We will kick it down the stairs. Then carry it towards the car."

"What if people see us?"

"No one will see us! Everyone is asleep!"

"FUCK! FUCK! FUCK!" Axel kept pacing back and forth, with both of his hands behind his neck.

"We will cover him with the sheets," I reassured Axel out of breath. Tears kept streaming down my face. I was still hyperventilating. "Its 4AM! No one should be out and about! We will be fine."

"Do you want to risk it?" Axel asked.

I stood up and looked at Father Orlando's dead corpse. *I want to fucking kick that body down the stairs!* "Yes."

Axel and I pushed the bulky and obese corpse down the staircase. The body loudly thumped on each stair. It reached the ground floor with great force. Axel sprinted towards the ground floor of the house.

"Get the white sheets!" Axel shouted from downstairs.

I sprinted towards Father Orlando's bedroom and got the blood-splattered white sheets that were scattered all over the mattress. This was the first time I had murdered someone. I didn't know what I was doing. I wasn't a professional at this. I ran down the stairs and handed the sheets to Axel.

"Go clean yourself!" Axel shrieked, "Get rid of the blood on your face! Quick!"

I bolted towards the bathroom of the ground floor of the house.

I looked deeply into the mirror. Blood streamed down the cheeks of my face. I had blood on my hands. I looked deeply within myself. I smiled. It had finally hit me. I was never going to regret it ever in my life. This was the moment that was going to change my life forever. I smiled at myself once again. I filled my hands with water from the sink and splashed it onto my face. I scrubbed my face harshly with soap, trying to get rid of all the blood that was splattered across my nose, cheeks, and forehead. I grabbed the hand towel beside the sink and dried my face out. I checked my hands. They were finally clean. I checked my face. My face had never looked that good ever before. It was the post-murdering glow. I fixed my hair. *'Oh, you look handsome.'* I was no longer upset or horrified. I was satisfied. I could feel the thrill and rush travelling through my organs. I had never felt this happy.

I walked towards the living room. Father Orlando's corpse was already wrapped in white sheets. It looked like a massive dirty laundry job. A dirty laundry job full of blood that had to be taken away from a house at 4AM to the trunk of a car.

"Okay. I'm going to go and open the trunk of the car," Axel nervously explained, "after I come back we are going to have to carry the body as fast as we can towards the trunk of the car. And FUCKING LEAVE!!!"

"Okay."

Axel rushed out of the house towards the cherry-red Jetta that was parked right in front of it.

I stayed with the deceased body. I was observing Father Orlando's body wrapped in the blood-splattered white sheets. He looked like a mummy. I couldn't stop staring at it. It was beautiful. A work of art. The best piece of art I had ever created.

Axel opened the door of the house. "Are you ready?!"

"Ready!" I replied.

Axel moved towards the other end of the body. "I'll grab him by the feet, you grab him by the head." Axel grasped the lower part of the body.

I grabbed the upper part of the body.

"Okay, one, two, three," Axel muttered. We both carried the body upwards.

"FUCK! This is heavy!" I loudly clamoured.

"Let's go! Now!" Axel howled.

We were both outside the house, on the porch, with a dead body in our hands.

"Close the door behind you!" Axel whispered.

I kicked the door shut with my leg.

Axel and I went down the wooden stairs of the porch with the deceased corpse. We looked on both sides. This had to be one of the scariest things I had ever done in my life. Thankfully, everyone was still asleep. The streets were still as silent as before. There were no lights coming from inside any of the houses. But the streetlights were still bright and beaming and could expose us at any given time.

This corpse was the heaviest thing my body had ever carried in my life. It was straining my muscles. But Axel was strong and powerful. He was the one doing most of the job. We walked towards the trunk of the cherry-red Jetta. But moments before arriving, I lost my strength. I accidentally let go of the body. The corpse noisily fell to the ground.

"FUCK!" Axel screeched.

"I'm sorry."

"WHAT THE FUCK TONY?" Axel screamed. I had never seen him this angry ever before.

"Fuck, fuck, let's carry him again!" *'We were definitely not trained professionals.'* I took hold of his bombarded head. "One, two, three…"

We carried the body again and walked towards the trunk of the cherry-red Jetta as fast as we could. Anyone could have caught us right in the moment.

We dumped the body onto the trunk. The sound of the body dropping into the trunk was loud and boisterous. Menacingly disturbing. This was worse than the crimes Bonnie and Clyde had ever committed.

"Let's go! Let's go!" Axel hollered, shutting the door of the trunk vigorously.

Axel ran onto the front seat of the car. I went the other way and got inside the car.

"The keys, where the fuck are my keys??!!" Axel exclaimed, patting his shorts, "FUCK!!"

"AXEL, COME ON!" I screamed, stressed for my life.

Axel looked down at the floor. "They're here! —"

"Turn the fucking car on!" I uttered.

Axel turned the engine on. The car felt heavier than usual. We had a dead body in the trunk of the car. But not just any dead body. We had Father Orlando's.

"GET OUT OF THIS ROAD NOW!" I cried out.

Axel surged out of McArdle Road at full speed.

It was 5:30AM. The mission was not over yet. We had to dispose of the body before leaving for Mexico first. The time pressure was still on. We had to be as quick and volatile as we could. Axel was driving at full throttle behind the stirring wheel. We were already miles away from McArdle Road.

"Where the fuck did you say you wanted to dump him?" Axel asked highly distressed.

"In the 'Rio del Rosario'! —"

"Where the fuck is that?"

"Under the mountain… near *the cross on top of the mountain!*"

"Oh, right yeah, yeah!"

Axel changed gear. And abruptly shifted the car towards his left. We were heading to the 'Rio del Rosario' next.

We arrived at the 'Rio del Rosario' at 6AM. It was dawn. The sun began to rise. Axel parked at the end of the river beneath the cliff of the mountain. A few kilometres away from where Jimmy threw himself off onto the highway. Axel and I got out of the car. The rapids and torrents of the river were strong and violent. The white waters were merciless and brutal. The river was long and broad, with an array of rocks and broken branches scattered throughout. We were in the middle of nature. There was no one else to be found, except coyotes and cougars. But I still had a gun in my pocket to protect us from anything.

"Okay, I'm going to open the trunk of the car." Axel put the car brake on.

"Yes."

"We carry the body and dump it into the river. After that we get in the car, and I'll get us into the 77 as fast as I can."

"Okay." My heart was still beating fast. My body was in survival mode. There was no time to ponder or think. There was just time to act.

Axel opened the trunk of the car. Father Orlando's corpse lied there wrapped in blood-splattered white sheets.

"Okay, grab him by the feet – I'll grab him by the head." Axel sprinted towards the other end of the body. "One, two, three…"

We both grabbed the body from each end. The body was heavier than before. I loudly grunted; the body was unbearable to carry. Axel was struggling too, but he knew that he had to get this job done as fast as he could.

We arrived at the edge of the river. The water was rushing swiftly between the rocks. The currents were fierce and savage. The river was going to mutilate and dismember Father Orlando's corpse. It was going to help us eradicate it from existence.

"One, two, three," Axel muttered, "NOW!"

We swayed the corpse back and forth and tossed it towards the river. "SPLASH!" Cold water sprinkled onto our bodies. We had just been hellishly baptised by the Devil. The body dived deep into the water like a huge bomb. The sound of the splash was excruciatingly loud. Axel hurriedly ran towards the car. But I stayed there. I wanted to say goodbye to the corpse. The body floated back to the surface after a short while. The body and the white sheets had already separated from each other. I saw Father Orlando's dead body rush through the rapids of the river, thumping on each stone and rock. I could still see the fear on his eyes. Like a zombie, his eyes were cloudy and bloodshot red. The body briskly swam all the way to the other end of the river until I could no longer see it. I was mystified and hypnotized. Captivated by how the water took his body away. Tears kept streaming down my eyes. It had finally been done. I had finally let him go. I had finally exterminated his shadow. I had never experienced that level of euphoria, fervent contentment and intense satisfaction in my life ever before.

"TONY! LET'S GO!" Axel screamed from the distance, "NOW!" Axel got inside of the driver's seat of the car.

I looked up at *the cross on top of the mountain*. The cross I had seen from the window of my room ever since I was a child. The cross that saw Jimmy fall off from the cliff into the freeway. The cross that voyeuristically watched how Father Orlando raped me. The cross that had witnessed all the crimes and violations that Corpus Christi and God had done to me. This was the last goodbye. This was the last time I was ever going to see that rusted iron cross.

I ran towards the car. I jumped into the passenger seat of the car and closed the door.

"Ready to go?" Axel agitatedly asked.

"Yes! Let's get the fuck out of here!"

Axel started the engine as fast as he could. He quickly put his foot on the pedal, changed gear and accelerated at maximum velocity. We drove out of the 'Rio del Rosario' at the speed of light creating a sandstorm behind us.

***

It was 8:30AM. We had been driving on the US-77 for about two hours now. We were miles away from Corpus Christi, making our way to Mexico. The scenery was breathtaking. The sky was bright baby blue. The clouds looked like turquoise-silver-hued cotton candy fluffs. There was an immense land of desert in each side of the highway. The land was filled with desiccated dried up brown grass and golden American dirt. The sun was neon yellow bright. The most beautiful morning light I had ever seen in my life. We were edging Raymondville, which was about two hours away from Matamoros, Mexico. I could already see the majestical gloriously carved mountains of Mexico in the distance. The radio was on. 'Long Cool Woman (In a Black Dress)' by The Hollies played at full volume. Axel had one hand on the stirring wheel, the other one on my left hand, gripping it tightly. I had suddenly forgotten I had just killed someone hours before. The weight Father Orlando had over me was no longer there. This was a dream. I had finally gotten rid of the shadow that had been following me my entire life. This was what self-governing dreams were made of. This was what happiness tasted like. The tension had dissipated from the air. The nervousness and anxiety had been left back in Corpus Christi. There was nothing to worry about anymore. The man I wanted to live with for the rest of my life was holding my hand firmly. Driving me to live the rest of our lives in Mexico. Away from my abusive mother and far away from the town that had destroyed me time after time. The windows of the car were open, wind rushed inside the car. I felt clean. I felt relieved. I felt alleviated. It felt like a wound had been healed. The wound that had been bleeding for so many years had finally scarred into a scab. I swayed my hair back and forth, rocking to the music that played in the radio. I let myself free, dashing my arms into the air, putting my head outside the window. Screaming into the desert.

"FUCK YOUUUUUU!!" I shouted at the top of my lungs, with my head poking out of the window. I laughed and had a big smile on my face.

Axel looked back at me and smiled. He was happy too. He was happy to see me content. He felt satisfied as well. He felt relieved that even though he couldn't kill his own abuser in the past, he helped me kill mine.

I reached towards the left pocket of my Realtree Camo pants and felt some keys dangling all the way in the bottom of my pocket. I took them out. They were my house keys. I looked at them closely. I gripped them tightly with both of my hands and fingers. They felt heavy. I pondered for a second. I thought about Mother and Father. I thought about Mario and Quique. I thought about the church I grew up in. I thought about my childhood. I thought about Father Orlando. I thought about the guy that raped me in 'The Texan Drive In'. I thought about Jimmy. I thought about Corpus Christi. I breathed in and out deeply and tossed them out of the window into the highway. This was the beginning of a new chapter in my life. I had finally said goodbye to Corpus Christi permanently.

I reached for Axel's right hand and looked up at him. "I love you."

He looked back at me for a second, engrossing my hand even tighter. "I love you even more."

XII

Motel Paraiso

Ezekiel 11:19

"I will give them an undivided heart and put a new spirit in them; I will remove from them their heart of stone and give them a heart of flesh."

We arrived in Mexico yesterday. We were staying at a cheap motel between the intersection of 'La Carretera 2' and 'La Carretera 180' in Matamoros, Tamaulipas. The place was called 'Motel Paraiso'. Coincidentally, we ended up in a motel called paradise. And after all the shit that Axel and I had gone through in our past, we had finally reached to our own version of utopia and heaven. We no longer had the shadows of our abusers creeping over us. We no longer were stuck in Corpus Christi. We no longer were in Texas. We no longer were in America. We were in *Paradise*.

The room of the motel was small. The beige paint on the walls was peeling. The ceiling fan spun at great speed, making a lot of noise. The blue navy duvet cover of the bed was rough and coarse. The polyester white sheets underneath smelled like sweat and humidity. The carpeted floor was full of stains and big brown blobs. There was no wall between the bathroom area and the bedroom. The double bed was in front of a white-tiled shower bath. The toilet and sink were right next to it. The room was lit with stark yellow, fluorescent lights. There was an old television beside the bed that played Mexican news and trashy telenovelas. There was mould growing in the corners of the room. And there was water damage on the ceiling above the bed. The place was certainly not appealing or inviting. It was the opposite. It was dirty and grotesque. But that didn't matter because Axel and I were happy.

It was 9:22AM. Or at least that was what the digital clock on the nightstand beside me said. Axel was still asleep. I stared at the ceiling, observing how the fan rapidly moved in circles. I could hardly sleep last night. I couldn't stop thinking about the fear Father Orlando had in his eyes moments before I killed him. I had already washed his blood from my hands, but it felt like his blood was going to stain me forever. Even though I felt satisfied, I was going to have to deal with this guilt for the rest of my life now. But maybe there was no room for guilt. Maybe there was no room for remorse. Father Orlando took my life first and that was the reason why I took his. Because that is how mother nature and the world works, you get what you deserve. I had never been a firm believer of karma, but the murder of Father Orlando was a great example of how karma worked to my own benefit. Somehow, I felt lighter. The weight I had been carrying on my shoulders all my life had suddenly been removed. And getting used to that lightness was definitely going to take me some time.

Axel opened his eyes and tossed his left arm around my chest. He pulled me towards him. He tightly wrapped his body around mine. He put his hairy legs over my hips. This was love. This was pure innocent juvenile love. I closed my eyes and took the moment in. The thoughts that had been spiralling inside my mind all night had magically disappeared. Nothing mattered anymore. Because the only thing I cared about now was Axel. This was the moment I had been waiting for my entire lifetime. The moment where I realized I was going to be able to spend the rest of my existence with the love of my life. The moment where I realized I was going to be able to go to sleep on Axel's chest every night and wake up with his arms around my body every morning until the day of my death. The moment where I realized I was never going to see Mother ever again. And the moment where I realized Father Orlando no longer breathed the same oxygen I did. I started to feel an exuberant immensity of light flowing throughout my body. I had mistaken my thrill, happiness and excitement with anxiety. Everything felt new and different, and although it was hard to gauge and process everything all at once, Axel's arms gripped around my chest grounded me into reality.

Axel gave me a kiss on my neck. "Good morning," he amorously said, with his stinky morning breath.

"Good morning," I turned around and kissed him on the lips, "or should I say, *Buenos Dias!*"

He laughed. "Were you able to sleep well?"

"Not really."

"Aww baby," he placed his forehead on mine, "don't worry, you're here now."

"Yes," I placed my hand on his cheek, "I love you."

"I love you more."

"No, *I love* you more," I countered.

"That is not possible. *I* love you EVEN more."

"FUCK NO! *I* love you more than you can ever think," I childishly played with his cheeks.

He grabbed me by the waist tightly, "You fucker!"

"What???" I laughed.

He passionately clutched the back of my neck and gave me a long-lasting kiss. Our lips were beautifully intertwined. Our tongues ludicrously duelled one another whilst both of our hands aggressively wrestled. The fervent love and passion felt more intense than ever. The fire that we both had started in Corpus Christi had become a catastrophic atomic bomb. Axel jumped on me and started to kiss me even more wildly than before. He pulled my long thick locks, and traced a curved and twisted line from my lower chin to my chest with his corrosive tongue. He crudely sucked on my nipples. I moaned. He looked up at me whilst he sucked them. I could see the earnest aggression and hostility in his eyes. I loved it. He licked my abdomen, flooding my stomach with his saliva. He took my boxers off. My erection slung into the air. He stroked my penis back and forth with his strong manly hands. He grabbed my legs and thighs and pinned them up against my chest. He buried his face on my ass. I whimpered. He licked the edges of my rectum. He put his tongue inside my asshole. The wetness of his tongue tickled me. I could feel his rough prickly stubble on the inner part of my ass cheeks. It felt good. After a few moments, he moved up to my face once again and kissed me even more. I could taste the sweat of my ass cheeks on my lips. He clutched my wrists and held them together with one hand. He smelled my sweaty hairy armpits and devoured them. I had never felt more pleasure than that ever in my life. This man worshipped me. I was his favourite possession.

He took his boxers off and gloriously grabbed his big fat cock. He pushed it into my face. He harshly slapped the cheeks of my face with the tip of his penis. I opened my mouth wide open. He mouth fucked me. He pulled my hair from the back of my head and spat inside my mouth. I wanted him to fuck me really bad. I wanted him to destroy me. I wanted him to be inside of me. I wanted him to emasculate me. I wanted him to take me to another dimension.

Axel fucked me as hard as he could inside the shower. Water roughly rained from the shower head onto the bathtub. Axel pushed me onto the mouldy, white-tiled wall of the shower. This was the hardest he had ever banged me. Axel put his hands on my mouth and bit my ears from behind. I could hear his zoomorphic grunting. Like primitive animals, we both feasted on each other. Both of our souls had left our bodies. This was an astral dream. An out-of-body experience. We were possessed by the post-murder high. There was something about Mexico that just made the sex even better. I had finally married the Devil. And life with the Devil was much better than the life I had with God before. He kept impaling the back of my ass with his feisty penis. We were making a mess. We were flooding the whole carpeted floor. Axel nailed his bony stringent chin on my collarbone. I took hold of his face with my left hand and scratched him out of pleasure and pain. I was jacking off with my right hand. The water was hot, and our bedroom was getting steamy. Fog consumed the whole space.

Axel slipped his penis out of me. "Get on your knees, baby," Axel grunted, "quick!"

I got on my knees and looked up at him. All I could see was the immensity and thickness of his dick.

Axel came all over my face. Semen dripped all over my eyelids and cheeks. He leaned down and licked the cum out of my face. We kissed and interchanged his bodily fluids with our tongues. Water kept pouring from the shower head onto us aggressively. We were happy.

We were both lying on the bed bare naked. I lied my head on his warm chest. I liked the sound of his heartbeat. I liked to feel the pressure of the blood pumping in and out of his heart, and how it made his left pectoral move closer to the left cheek of my face. He played with my wet hair. These were the kind of moments I wanted to last forever. I didn't want time to pass. I wanted time to freeze.

"What do you want to do today?" Axel asked.

"I don't know…" I looked up at him.

Axel kept playing with my hair, running his fingers between my dampened locks.

"I can't believe we are here…"

"I know. It feels surreal," Axel looked down at me, "it doesn't feel real."

I moved my hand towards his face. "I want to live the rest of my life with you."

"Me too."

"This is the happiest I have ever been—" I smiled.

"Tony—"

"Yes?"

"Thank you."

"Thank you for what?" I laughed.

"For everything."

"What do you mean?" I was slightly confused.

"I don't know," he sighed, "it feels like I've let a part of me go when you killed Father Orlando." He paused for a second. "I feel better. I feel lighter. I feel like I almost killed my own uncle in a way."

I beamed. I squeezed his cheeks even tighter with both of my hands.

"You are so brave," he said.

"So are you."

Axel was staring at the ceiling. He was lost in his thoughts.

"I wouldn't have been able to do it without you," I mentioned.

Axel looked back at me. "You are the best thing that has ever happened to me."

My eyes started to water. No one had ever said that to me. I no longer felt worthless. That was exactly what I had been waiting to hear my entire life. "I love you," I whispered.

"Not again! —" he caterwauled.

"Are you not going to say, 'I love you' back???"

"No, because then we will never be able to agree on who loves each other more."

"You are right." I looked up at his beautiful jade green eyes. They were mesmerising and hypnotizing. There were a million galaxies and universes hidden inside the irises around his pupils. His smell. His touch. I loved every single bit of this man. "Axel?"

"Yeah?" he muttered.

"I think I know what I want to do today…"

"What?"

"I think I want to shave my head." I looked at him for reassurance and approval, knowing very well that he was going to disapprove of this mad and sickening idea.

"What?" he audibly laughed, "Why??!"

"I don't know…" I ran my fingers through my own wet hair, "I want to feel lighter."

"But your beautiful long hair—"

"I knowww… But I want to let go of my past… I want to let go of all the trauma that has been stuck in the follicles of my hair for this long—"

"But if you do, I won't be able to pull the back of your head when I fuck you anymore—" he jokingly babbled.

"AXEL!"

"It *is* true though," he giggled like a little kid.

"I want *you* to shave my head," I looked at him with puppy eyes.

Axel paused for a moment. He grabbed my hair and touched it. He didn't seem very convinced. But he wanted to do whatever made *me* happy. "Okay," Axel shook my hair frantically with both of his hands, "let's do it then! It's going to be fun!"

"Okay!"

Axel leaned in for a kiss. I countered it with an even bigger kiss. I put my hands behind his neck and wrapped myself around him. We started to make out again.

Axel and I browsed the 'Mercado Gonzalez' supermarket like little kids in a toy store. The supermarkets in Mexico were even bigger than the ones in America. Everything was extremely cheap. The fruit and vegetables looked ripe and fresh. The packaged food seemed slightly healthier. But like the motel, the supermarket wasn't appealing to the eye either. The floor was made from dirty cement; it was filthy and sticky. The air smelled like rotten fish and laundry detergent. The blinking lights above us were bright and vivid and exposed every little flaw of the place. We looked foreign. We were the black sheep in the herd. It was the first time we had left the motel in Mexico. We came to steal food and to try to find an electric hair clipper to shave my head. Axel looked through the hair product aisle. I walked behind him whilst I zipped up my backpack. I had filled it with canned food, chocolate bars and bags of chips to the brim.

"How are you getting on?" Axel quietly asked.

"Got a few things in my bag."

"Good. I got a few stuff on mine too."

"We are so good at this," I subtly laughed.

"It's easier to do it here than in America," Axel whispered.

"I know," I looked back at the aisle, "I don't even know who works here."

"I'm trying to look for your hair clipper," Axel muttered.

"Should we ask?"

"Oh, nope. It's here!" Axel pointed to a caged glass box filled with clippers, trimmers, and hair straighteners.

"Oh shit. It's locked."

"We are going to have to pay for it," Axel rolled his eyes.

"We are going to have to ask someone to come unlock it then—"

"How much is it?" Axel apathetically asked.

"329."

"329! —" Axel exclaimed.

"329 Pesos… Not dollars… Don't worry… I don't know how much that is in dollars though…"

"For fuck's sake Tony."

"I'm sure they'll take our dollars!" I padded Axel's lower back, "Come on! Go get someone!"

Axel dramatically sighed like a spoiled bratty child who was about to throw a tantrum.

"Go on!" I youthfully squealed.

Axel walked off in the distance.

I loudly laughed like a hyena across the aisle.

He looked back at me.

I winked at him and mischievously giggled.

The muffled sound of the television consumed the whole space. The flickering light that came from the TV lit the entire room. It was a hot night. The windows were wide open, and the wind that came from the highway rustled through the cheap white linen motel curtains. There were beer cans on the floor. Bags of chips and chocolate wrappers were scattered all throughout the room as well. I sat on a cheap plastic chair in front of the mirror and the sink. I was shirtless, with my long curly brown hair exposed. Axel and I had been drinking all night. We had been having a good time. Axel stood behind me with a wired electric hair clipper on his right hand.

"Are you ready?" he cautiously asked.

"Oh fuck!" I shut my eyes really tight.

"What??" Axel cackled.

"I don't know if I want to do it anymore."

"Tony!" Axel shrieked, "You made me pay for it! —I'm going to fucking give you a buzz cut now! —"

"Okay, okay, okay…" I looked down at my hands. They were nervously shaking. "Just give me a second."

"Okay," he said, resting the hair clipper on my shoulder.

I looked at myself in the mirror. This was it. This was going to be the death of the old Tony. This was the moment when I decided to move on from the past. This was the moment when I decided I *wasn't* going to allow my traumas and hardship to dictate my life anymore. This was the moment when I decided I wanted to start to live again.

I had always thought that hair clung to many things. It clung to the bad memories. Like a metal conductor, it would cling to the experiences that had hurt you the most. I was ready for a fresh start. I was ready to shave my head and start all over again. I was ready to take control of myself once more and reclaim my own narrative.

I looked at Axel through the mirror and pondered for a second. The summer of 1996 had been the hottest American summer on record since 1974. But the summer of 1996 had also been the summer that had changed my life forever. I breathed in and out solemnly. I looked at myself in the mirror again. I smiled.

"I'm ready," I confidently uttered.

Axel switched the corded electric hair clipper on. He started to shave me from the top of my forehead to the back of my head. I could feel the buzz in my skull. I could feel the shivers in my spine. I could feel the blood rushing into my cheeks. I could feel the thrill and excitement inside my body. Big clumps of hair fell onto the dirty carpeted floor. Like a white swan feather, I started to feel even lighter than before.

I was a phoenix rising from the ashes. Leaving everything behind.

Ephesians 6:12

"For our struggle is not against flesh and blood,
but against the rulers, against the authorities,
against the powers of this dark world and
against the spiritual forces of evil in the heavenly realms."

AFTERWORD

Untitled Reflection
by Iñaki Aguilar Lomelí

I lost sight of it all one day. My body was trembling, my bones were achy and rather cold. I was feeling a little bit too weak, my stomach was already unemployed. My legs were out of work, physically unable to go switch the heating on. All of the fires that used to keep me warm once, had left me unknown and forgotten all the way in the back of the fridge.

It all just came into fruition that one night, in my room all alone around 2:49. Your scrawny knuckles bruising the inside of my skull, infused with the pain you used to cause me when your teeth used to scrape my chest, and your saliva would erode the skin and centre of my venter.

Scrolling through my phone, all bored, these fucking miserable apps. Airing your messages, ignoring your calls, I wanted to wipe you out of my world. To heavily drain you out of my system. I wish I could've been brave enough to grab something sharp next to my bed in order to leak my veins and erase your face and name from my brain.

I wish I could wake up one day with someone calling me about your death.

But why would I want to wish death upon someone who didn't do anything wrong? What if I am liable for this pain and turmoil? Maybe you are not the one to blame when we go off the rails. Maybe I am the evil warlock who shapeshifted you into all of my traumas and insecurities. Maybe you didn't deserve this. Maybe you didn't deserve to be blamed for my starving and my compulsive running.

Maybe I should start blaming myself.

I let all these men exploit me just so I could forget about you. I let someone crash me into a tree and choke me just so I could forget the touch and taste of you.

But I always let this happen. I like being pushed to the ground; I like being degraded like I'm not enough. I try to stand up, trusting myself that I will never let anyone do this again, but the knife is too shiny and so beautifully sharp to not stab my own chest once again.

We started to bathe in blood, and when I mistakenly bloviated 'I love you', you were unable to speak or move. I saw you fall on somebody else's skin like a disloyal flower bud which had given their nectar to far too many greedy bees.

Now that you're gone, and you've left. I am just 'a bag of skin and bones' or at least that is what my mum screamed in the corridors of my house when she walked on me undressing in my room.

I wish I could've told you how scary it was to faint in public. What it felt like to daze off and start losing your vision and hearing. To let your body fall to the ground, and wake up and see a dozen people waiting around your body to see if you were still alive.

But when I opened my eyes, you were sadly not there.

Now I step on the scale every day just to see if I'm one pound lighter and breathe deep enough in front of the mirror just to see, admire, and caress my bulging ribs.

I kiss older men in the club, and they bring me back to their lavishly dressed houses. They like to fuck me like their toys beneath their beds. They clutch and hold my body like one of their other many expensive acquisitions. They let me walk around their living rooms naked and allow me to touch their trophies and gold-rim glasses. I wear their so-called silk Versace robes and steal cash from their wallets.

I post about them online and block them from my stories. All I want is some sort of attention, I pose with their BAFTAs and filmic awards. But I'm kind of unable to speak about the way they actually held me, hostage, in their bed post that night, cutting circulation with a cincture around my wrists.

'I'm so tired of getting abused.' I often think when I am all crumbled up in the corner of my room. But then again, I never know how to fight back or let go. Sometimes it's just easier to close my eyes and think of something else. Let them cause damage, let them fulfil their sinful deeds and wreak havoc. I remind myself I can cry about it later to the plants in my washroom or attempt to suppress it on the dance floor. Like a vicious circle letting another one of those mongrels do the exact same thing the next night.

Is this what I think I deserve?

Because when I was fifteen and depressed, my therapist locked his office and asked me to undress. He touched, massaged, and breathed on me. Asked me to touch myself down there and give him a show. I can still smell his awful stench on the follicles of my hair, and his fingertips tainted in my skin, which I have crudely attempted to cover up with meaningless tattoos. I tried to get a snake one, maybe that way, one day, I will be able to shed the skin he once tarnished.

I still want to kill him to death, to this very day.

I downed a peanut butter jar last night whilst taking a bath and purged it in the toilet right beside it. I slept on my right side, trying to avoid the feeling and sensation of your osseous chin nailing the surface of my collarbone. I listen to sad music on my way back home after my shift and purposefully cry in front of people in the tube just to get a 'are you okay?' from someone. Everyone is a little bit too busy nowadays, I seem to forget.

You think you are twenty and you still haven't found the love of your life, but all I do is ponder whether I am good enough or not when I have some male's arms wrapped around my waist.

Why do all these men keep causing the same kind of pain?

When did the euphoria of starvation become the male validation, I have so long craved when I was eight and my brother kicked me with a football on my face because I wanted to wear my sister's pink lace dress?

Men keep hurting other men, I still remember the dust and grime on my face after those drunk football men pushed me onto the pavement and pledged my neck in front of the discotheque.

All these perceptions and opinions, the soft dainty boys with their books and skinny looks moulded my body into a gear I could barely walk with. Can somebody please tell me where does justice lie in that?

Is it even worth smiling when your ribs are protruding from the sides of your stomach, unable to physically laugh, and you just keeping lying about your breakfast time and a half?

All my friends tend to love this 'unified' community and like pawns, they move strategically in this intricate and complicated chess game. They go to these clubs and dance and fuck, and fuck and dance. All these men want is someone's frail body to destroy. One of them blatantly bawling at me with their boozed-up breath, "If you don't want to be objectified or sexualised by other men then you shouldn't be posting your naked body online."

I want to be desired, to be liked, to be craved. Scared that if I go thick or if the number on the scale goes up men will be unable to see me past my figure and throw my rotten bones in an elephant's graveyard like a toddler dissatisfied with their meal.

I want to be accepted, but at what cost?

Lately, I've started to eat more, but I cry when I feel full. I squeeze my belly and try to deflate it with my feisty nails. I have stopped counting the calories but am somehow unable to stop running the kilometres.

I still steal shit from the counters and hide it under my puffer. I am deemed sinful and corrupt for committing a crime, but what is the crime in trying to dismantle a society that has already deemed you as being worthless and despicable enough your entire life?

Where is the fun in life if you don't live for the thrill and fear of getting caught? Like loving someone so much that you forget who you are and let the tides of their voyeuristic oceans drown you in the depths of your own inner self-sabotage machinery.

I always thought I needed to add another person or man to my equation. But after many muddy lonely walks in Hampstead

Heath, I have realised that I ought to subtract that idyllic nonsense shit I see on social occasions from my life.

Maybe the love story I need is not necessarily the one I want.

Maybe that love story, the one I keep looking for, waiting for me all the way at the end of the tunnel, includes no one else, but *my own self.*

Iñaki Aguilar Lomelí
February 21st, 2023

William Shakespeare, Othello

*"It is silliness to live when to live is torment;
and then have we a prescription to die
when death is our physician."*

———————————

Available worldwide from Amazon

_____

Michael Terence
Publishing

www.mtp.agency

www.facebook.com/mtp.agency

@mtp_agency